John Davidson

Godfrida

A Play in Four Acts

John Davidson

Godfrida
A Play in Four Acts

ISBN/EAN: 9783743389953

Manufactured in Europe, USA, Canada, Australia, Japa

Cover: Foto ©Andreas Hilbeck / pixelio.de

Manufactured and distributed by brebook publishing software
(www.brebook.com)

John Davidson

Godfrida

GODFRIDA

A PLAY IN FOUR ACTS

BY JOHN DAVIDSON

JOHN LANE: THE BODLEY HEAD

NEW YORK AND LONDON

1898

𝕌niversity 𝕻ress:

JOHN WILSON AND SON, CAMBRIDGE, U. S. A.

PROLOGUE

INTERVIEWER
POET

Interviewer. I understand you are about to publish a play which you have written for the stage.

Poet. Yes.

Interviewer. Pardon me, but do you think it wise to publish a play before it has been produced?

Poet. I intend to produce it before publication.

Interviewer. Ah, yes; to secure the dramatic rights. But I mean that people will not read a play which they have not seen.

Poet. I would not care to invite an audience to witness a play which I could not invite my readers to peruse.

Interviewer. Well. — Is it in verse?

Poet. Principally. There is some prose dialogue.

Interviewer. Then is it a continuation of your attempt to revive the Jacobean poetic drama?

Poet. My attempt to do so? I never made such an attempt.

Interviewer. I understood you had done so in your early plays, just as· you attempted lately to revive the Elizabethan eclogue.

Poet. Nothing was further from my mind than either revival. My endeavour was always to write Victorian plays, Victorian eclogues.

Interviewer. Then, do you assure me that your early plays were written for the stage?

Poet. I had the stage in my mind, but constantly lost sight of it, except in " Scaramouch in Naxos ; " it I hope to see performed some day.

Interviewer. But is not verse on the stage a lapse from modernity — a backsliding?

Poet. I think not.

Interviewer. You have expressed somewhere in your writings an intense admiration of Ibsen. Will his influence be found in your play?

Poet. I think not.

Interviewer. Have you ceased to admire Ibsen?

Poet. Oh, no! I share the opinion of those who regard him as the most impressive writer of his time, as the most expert playwright, and most original dramatist the world has seen.

Interviewer. But you are not a disciple?

Poet. No; nothing comes of discipleship except misinterpretation. That seems to me the history of all schools.

Interviewer. But if Ibsen is as great as you say, would it not be wise to follow in his steps?

Poet. No; it would be as foolish, as it is unnecessary, to attempt to do over again what Ibsen has done.

Interviewer. Can you not extend the path he has laid down, then?

Poet. No; any step forward from Ibsen would land me in some mystical abyss, or some slough of Naturalism. For me Ibsen is the end, not the beginning.

Interviewer. Do you propose your own play as a new beginning?

Poet. No. Before I sat down to write " Godfrida " I read over my early plays, and the lot was cast for Romance.

Interviewer. What do you mean by Romance?

Poet. A pertinent question. I mean by Romance the essence of reality. Romance does not give the bunches plucked from the stem : it offers the wine of life in chased goblets. I have moulded and carved my goblet to the best of my art; and I have crushed wine into it. To leave this Euphuism, I take men and women as I know them — the brain-sick, ISEMBERT, ERMENGARDE; the healthy, GODFRIDA, SIWARD; but that I myself may realise them, and make them more apparent and more engaging to an audience, I place them in an imaginary environment, and in the colour and vestments of another time.

Interviewer. What is the main idea of your play? Can you tell?

Poet. It has been my companion long enough for that, I hope. You may find the poles of my play in this quotation : —

> ". . . no felicity
> Can spring in men, except from barbèd roots
> Of discontent and envy, deeply struck
> In some sore heart that hoped to have the flower,"

and in this, —

> " I have had a vision of the soul of life,
> And love alone is worthy."

Interviewer. What was your object in writing this play?

Poet. My object was to give delight.

Interviewer. Do you consider that a high aim?

Poet. I consider it the highest aim of art.

Interviewer. To give delight?

Poet. Yes; to give delight is to impart strength most directly, most permanently.

Interviewer. Is there anything else you wish to say about " Godfrida " ?

Poet. Yes. When I was a boy I knew by heart Kingsley's " Hereward the Wake," having read it every Sunday for several years in a bound volume of *Good Words.* As I developed my play a memory of " Hereward," which I did not recognise at first, besieged my fancy. Becoming conscious of its source, and being quite unable to get away from it, I obtained the kind permission of Kingsley's representatives to use it. The matter I have taken occupies a few paragraphs of the novel ; but it is important in the play.

Interviewer. When will it be produced in London ?

Poet. I have made no arrangements.

Interviewer. Thank you.

Poet. Good-day.

THE PERSONS OF THE PLAY

ISEMBERT . . . . *The Chancellor of Provence.*

SIWARD . . . . *The Constable of Provence.*

ADOMAR . . . . *A foolish person.*

CYPRIAN . . . . *Isembert's secretary.*

INGLERAM . . . . *Godfrida's uncle.*

DAGOBERT . . . . *Siward's predecessor in office.*

BERTHOLD . . . . *A drunkard.*

ANSELM
SCIPIO } . . . . *Pages to the Duchess.*

GAUCELM . . . . *Seneschal of the Palace.*

LUDOVIC . . . . *The Captain of the Guard.*

THANGBRAND . . . . *Siward's man.*

MARCABRUN
MELCHIOR } . . . . *Spadassins.*

The Lieutenant of the Guard.

ERMENGARDE . . . . *The Duchess of Provence.*

GODFRIDA.

CLARE . . . . *Godfrida's companion.*

Ladies and Gentlemen, Men-at-arms, Halberdiers and Servants.

TIME : *The middle of the Fourteenth Century.*

SCENE : *Provence. The first three acts take place in Arles on the forenoon, afternoon, and evening, respectively, of one day; the fourth act among the ruins of Theodoric's Castle at some distance from Arles on the evening of the day following.*

GODFRIDA

ACT I

SCENE. — *A room in Ingleram's house in Arles. At the back a large door opens into a garden. Through the trees in the garden glimpses of the horizon, a rolling wooded line, are seen. On the left of the garden the backs of other houses are visible. There are doors right and left, that on the left being well back. A broad latticed window at the back looks on the garden; a smaller one in a recess commands the street. The walls are hung with tapestry. In front on the right a table with four chairs set about it: a flask of wine and glasses are on the table. There is a seat in the recess; and on the window-sill several vellum-bound books. In front on the left a couch. Chairs on which are the hats of* INGLERAM, *etc., are set conveniently. A spinning-wheel near the large window. A summer morning.*

When the act-drop rises INGLERAM *is closing the door at the back; and* DAGOBERT *and* BERTHOLD *are seated at the table.* INGLERAM *is stout; grey hair, moustache, and pointed beard; about fifty; richly dressed.* BERTHOLD *is pouring out wine for himself; his hair is untidy, and he has a dissipated appearance; about thirty-five; his dress has been splendid, but is faded and stained.* DAGOBERT, *about thirty, lounges with his head on his hand; richly dressed.*

With the exception of GODFRIDA, INGLERAM, CLARE, *and the servants, the persons in this act enter and go out by the door on the left.*

Berthold. Cyprian is coming.

Ingleram [*sitting at the head of the table*]. He joins us, then.

Berthold. Yes.

Ingleram. I have not seen him since he returned from Algiers.

Berthold. He is the portrait of discontent. If he were the only creature left alive, I believe he would cut his own throat to be avenged on mankind.

Ingleram. He was shamefully neglected.

Berthold. More so than we imagined. He tells me

that besides his own venture, he sailed upon business for the Duchess herself when the Dey's galleys seized him.

Ingleram. And she would not ransom him!

Berthold. Oh, she promised! But the late Duke left the treasury at a low ebb; and then came the war with Esplandian to keep her coffers empty.

Ingleram. That will not solace Cyprian.

Berthold. No; it is difficult to console a man for a year's slavery; his very soul is tanned and wealed.

Dagobert. It puzzles me to think why Isembert should have paid his ransom.

Ingleram. Isembert, having climbed into the Chancellorship by the usual ladder of friends, kicked the ladder down in the usual way. Now, a man in power, if he has no friends, must have creatures; and so Isembert hopes he has bought Cyprian, body and soul.

Berthold. But I know better. Cyprian serves only his own ends; and that Lucifer will find.

Ingleram. Lucifer?

Berthold. His excellency, the Chancellor, Isembert the proud.

Ingleram. Proud is too good for him; an impudent, fantastical, spurious sort of genius. Provence is tired of him.

Dagobert. But why the devil is Cyprian late? We

shall see no part of the tournament if we have not our
talk over quickly.

Berthold. True. And the tournament will not see us,
which would set tongues wagging. I wonder if he is
near. [*Goes out and re-enters immediately.*] Here he
comes ! [*Sits and pours out wine for himself.*

Enter CYPRIAN. *He stands near the centre of the stage.
He is plainly dressed in dark garments ; his face is
almost black ; his hair grizzled. He has an inkhorn
and case of pens at his girdle.*

Ingleram [*rises and offers his hand.* CYPRIAN *gives
him a finger*]. Welcome back to Provence, Cyprian.
Our plot needed only you. You shall bring us luck ; fate
has some peculiar use for a man who is snatched from
the grave.

Cyprian. From a worse place.

Ingleram [*jocosely*]. Indeed, you have been singed.
[*Resumes his seat.*] Sit, Cyprian. We have little
time.

Cyprian [*doggedly*]. I must know more than Berthold has told me. I must know the individual roots of
your conspiracy. My own ill-will at the world is of the
simplest, the deepest. I thought myself as others do, a
careless, gallant fellow, capable of heroism — when there

is nothing else for it. A cut or two of the bastinado, and I howled out my recantation.

Dagobert. Forswore the cross!

Cyprian. And was despised for my pains; set to the most laborious and meanest employments: chained and scourged. If I know myself, I take my stand deliberately on the side of evil. My purse is empty; my misery fathomless. Your plot promises — to me, wealth; to Isembert, whom I hate for his arrogant appropriation of my life, ruin and despair; but before I sit with you I must know why you, and you, and you have become traitors: to secure myself against betrayal I must be certain that it is your pleasure to sacrifice the world's good opinion and your own self-respect.

Ingleram [uneasily]. Well —

Berthold [angrily]. Oh!

Dagobert. Bravely pronounced. [*Rises.*] You face
    the naked fact.
We 're ruined too, bankrupt in purse and soul.
Old Ingleram has spent his niece's dower;
Under the Duchess shame, imprisonment,
Perhaps a halter, lie in wait for him.
Berthold is deep in debt to Ingleram;
And for myself —

    Ingleram [starting up]. I shall account for you.

Our poor Dagobert — there's for your "old Ingleram"
— I say our simple Dagobert, as you know, was once
Constable of Provence. Surely that is reason enough
why he should avenge himself on Siward, a wandering
fellow, who changed defeat into victory, drove Esplandian over the border, and supplanted Dagobert in her
Grace's favour.

Dagobert. Eclipsed, abandoned, broken, thrust aside,
Except as traitors we are wholly lost.
Wealth, power, and vengeance will repay our crime
If to Esplandian we deliver up
The Duchess and her coveted Provence.

Cyprian. Yes. Well; I join you.   [*They all sit.*

Ingleram [*effusively*]. My dear Cyprian —

Cyprian. No hypocritical fellowship. We know what
we are. — Why will the Duchess not wed Esplandian?
That no one has ever told me. He is her cousin, and
the next heir. It would be a most politic union; besides,
it would deliver her from Isembert, at whose control she
begins to chafe.

Ingleram. There it is ! The late Duke urged the marriage on his death-bed; and that is Esplandian's excuse
for his former invasion, for the invasion which is pre-
paring, and for our policy.

Dagobert. Then he is much older than she; and, if

she were to wed him, she would become of no importance in the state, he being, as you say, the next heir, and an exceedingly crafty ruler. Moreover, she is resolved never to wed at all. In fact —

Berthold [*rises, impatiently*]. She is a woman, and will have her own way. [*Crosses to door on the left.*] I 'm for the tournament. There is no more to be said. Come, we shall be missed.

[*A general movement towards the left door.*

Cyprian. This will end, as it begins, with the spilling — of wine. You have no plot.

Ingleram. Nonsense! Esplandian has stolen across the Rhone already, and I expect an immediate message from him.

Enter ISEMBERT. *He is tall; clean-shaved; iron-grey hair hanging to his shoulders; between forty and fifty; richly dressed.*

Ingleram. The Chancellor!

Dagobert. Isembert!

Berthold [*swaggers up to* ISEMBERT *and offers his hand, which* IMSEBERT *declines*]. Most opportune! We four desperadoes, plotting some means of restoration to her Grace's favour, talked of you this very moment; and, you know, talk of the devil —

Isembert. And don't tell him too much of your mind.

         [*Crosses to* INGLERAM.

Berthold [*blustering after* ISEMBERT]. You disdain me, sir?

Isembert [*over his shoulder*]. I disdain your condition.

Berthold. By stoop and cup, sir, I would have you know that I can be brimful of wine and yet not drunk!

Isembert. So can a bottle. — Ingleram, I want you: [INGLERAM *bows stiffly. As the others seem indisposed to leave,* ISEMBERT *looks from them to the door on the left; and they go out,* DAGOBERT *jauntily, and* BER-THOLD *in a fume. As* CYPRIAN *goes out* ISEMBERT *gives him a significant glance, to which he replies with a nod.*] What keeps Godfrida from the tournament?

Ingleram. I wish I knew! Not her own will.

Isembert.   Whose then?

Ingleram. The Duchess flatly bade her stay at home.

   [ISEMBERT *walks across the stage in deep thought,*
     paying no heed to the rest of INGLERAM'S
     speech.]

It puzzles me. They were companions — friends
Since childhood ; daily·meetings, messages,
Letters and gifts cease suddenly, no cause
Assigned. — I am afraid I tire you.

Isembert.   No ;

I was n't listening.

    Ingleram.   Then what brings you here ?

    Isembert. I wish to see your niece.

    Ingleram.   Concerning what ?

    Isembert. I love her.

    Ingleram [*astonished*]. You among the fry of boys,
Of widowers, dotards, and adventurers
Who seek her for her fortune and her face !

    Isembert [*scornfully*]. Her fortune !

                         [*Goes up stage.*

    Ingleram [*to himself*]. Does he know? . . . What
      hope have you ?

    Isembert. The highest hope. This is the day the fate
Within me has appointed to disclose
The love that in Godfrida's heart and mine,
Unhidden though unuttered, waits my word.

    Ingleram. Godfrida is a girl, and you as old
Almost as I.

    Isembert.   Time is the earliest thrall
Enslaved by men who shape the world. My years
Are all attainments in Godfrida's eyes.

                [*Looking out at the back.*]

She has just now left the garden. Bid her come.

    Ingleram. This overweening style of yours to me !

Isembert. To you, sir. Bid her come.

> [*Comes down stage.*

Ingleram [*to himself*]. What does he know?

> [*Goes out at the back.*

ISEMBERT *crosses quickly to the door on the left,*
which he opens. Re-enter CYPRIAN.

Cyprian. You want me?

Isembert. Yes. Hide somewhere in the street.
When Ingleram has gone, return. [CYPRIAN *goes out.*]

> [*Re-enter* INGLERAM *from the garden.*]

> She comes?

Ingleram. After a little. She is with the maids.

Isembert. She is a famous housewife, I believe.
I shall await her here. Follow your friends. [INGLERAM
goes out surlily by the door on the left.]
This drudge was once a man! Ignoble aims
Meanly pursued would rot a hero's heart.

> [*Re-enter* CYPRIAN.]

Well; a conspiracy?

Cyprian. As you divined.
I am hand and glove with them to share the spoil
After Esplandian's [*ironically*] certain victory.

Isembert. They know Esplandian has crossed the
Rhone? [CYPRIAN *assents.*]
What is the arch — the keystone of their scheme?

Cyprian. 'T is all unhewn. They wait Esplandian's
  stroke.

Isembert. But Siward's prowess: have they counted
  that?

Cyprian. They have counted nothing but necessity —
Their debts, disgraces, losses, wounded pride.

Isembert. Well, we shall see. Back with you to the
  lists.
And not a word of this to Ermengarde:
If she should ask for me, say I am busy.

> [CYPRIAN *goes out.*

Enter GODFRIDA *from the garden; beautiful; twenty
  years old. She is grave on her entrance, but as soon
  as she sees* ISEMBERT *the cloud passes from her face.*

Godfrida. Oh, my lord Chancellor! My uncle said —
And doggedly refused the suppliant's name —
A hapless lover sought his *coup-de-grâce.*
Good-morning, Isembert.

Isembert [*holding her hand*]. I am tongue-tied
Before your beauty, now that I have come
To claim it for my own.

Godfrida [*withdraws her hand, amazed at first;
  then pleasantly*]. Well-acted, sir!
What part shall I play in your comedy?

2

Isembert. You . . . No! My love for you unknown
    to you?
Have you not watched and felt yourself become
The essence, the idea of my life?
Your eyes are branded on my heart; your voice
Stored in my hearing like a golden hoard;
The lustre of your presence gilds the world;
Your haunting memory lights my loneliness:
And I believed you loved me.

  Godfrida [*sadly*].   That was rash.
But men will still mistake good-will for love.

                        [*Goes up stage.*

  Isembert. You love me not! [GODFRIDA *is about to*
    go out.] Godfrida! [GODFRIDA *turns.*]   Hate
    me then.
This sorrow, this majestic tenderness
Disarms and baffles me. Be petulant;
Be scornful; sting my pride; then could I hate
And wound you with a scorpion-lash of words:
Give me your hate; for I must love or hate.

  Godfrida. But it is thanks I owe you, Isembert.
I think that love when it is love indeed
Exceeds in value everything besides:
When I shall love I hope for thanks at least.
Believe me, sir, I thank you from my heart.

                    [*Goes out at the back.*

Isembert [*sinks on the couch, then rises slowly*].

Must I distrust my passion and my hope,

The angels of my life, that ne'er till now

Misled me?   Can it be that like the ruck

Of humankind my passion and my hope

Are only lackeys to my vanity?

I know not what to do, or what to think!

This is defeat — for me, whose thoughts are deeds.

[*Goes up stage and looks out.*]

Already gone!   When in her heart she feels

And truly understands that I . . . Yes! Clare!

Enter CLARE *from the garden; about forty; calm and
   gentle, without the appearance of a dependant.*

Clare. Your excellency?

Isembert.   I shall come to-day again —

To-day.

Clare. To see my mistress, sir?

Isembert.   To-day —

After the tournament.   [*Goes out.*

CLARE *summons servants, who enter from the
      right and remove the flask and glasses.* GOD-
      FRIDA *re-enters from the right, and sitting in
      the window-seat becomes absorbed in a book.*

Clare.   The Chancellor

Will visit you to-day again, he says.

Godfrida. Indeed, I hope not, and I think not, Clare.

> [*When the servants have gone*, GODFRIDA *takes*
> *her book to the table and begins to pore over*
> *it.* CLARE *sits at the spinning-wheel.*

Clare. What are you reading?

Godfrida.   Magic, sorcery;
Of love-charms and of love.

Clare.   You are in love.

Godfrida [*startled*].   I never said it, Clare.

Clare.   No, but I know:
You are in love with Siward.

Godfrida.   What is this?
Siward? My champion is Sir Adomar.

Clare [*amused*].   Oh! Adomar!

Godfrida.   He wears my ribbon.

Clare.   True;
He is your valentine; but that is play:
You have not said three words to Adomar.

Godfrida. I have not said one word to Siward yet;
Nor met him; nor been near him.

Clare.   But your thoughts
Have parleyed: you remember when he rode,
After his first great victory, down the street,
How from your lattice — Oh, I watched you well! —
His eyes drank in a look of yours. And then

Your constant talks with Anselm, Siward's friend,
And yours — nothing but Siward and his deeds,
His beauty and his strength!

   Godfrida [*half angry, half happy*]. You witch! For
     shame!

I talk of whom I please.

   Clare.   Who pleases you.

   Godfrida. Does Anselm think I love this Norseman,
     then?

Clare, do they talk of this? Is this supposed?
I am a woman: I can veil my thoughts:
It cannot be; a child can hide her love.

   Clare. Not from a witch. A silly prating boy,
Like Anselm, sees it not; nor any one
Save me: your secret is your own and mine . . .
And Siward's too.

   Godfrida.   Impossible! — Clare? — Speak!

   Clare. If to Godfrida Anselm talks of Siward
In frankest innocence and boyish pride,
He talks to Siward of Godfrida too.
A soldier knows the world: in Anselm's looks
Fresh from your presence Siward sees a glass
That holds an image of your secret love.
And now I think of it, another knows:
Do you not guess why you are driven from court?

Godfrida. The Duchess's caprice. Thrice in a month
She has commanded me to keep the house.
She has the power, and treats me like a girl.

Clare. No more than that you think.

Godfrida.   What do you mean?

Clare. The tournament. To-day Siward will fight
And carry off the prize.

Godfrida.   I hope so. Well?

Clare. Why, every time you have been driven from
     court
Some festival or pageant was on foot.

Godfrida. What then?

Clare.   Siward and you have never met.

Godfrida. In God's name, cousin, tell me what you
     mean!

Clare. The Duchess Ermengarde is jealous of you.
It all grows clear to me now as we talk.

Godfrida. Jealous of me! Does she love Siward too?

Clare. You are her only rival in the land;
As rich, as beautiful, and people say
Sweeter, and of a nobler mind than she.

Godfrida. This cannot be! In love with Siward? No;
The Duchess means to live and die unwed;
Often she told me so when we were friends.
What friends we were too, Clare! But that is past.

During her reign I was to rule, she said :

She reigns ; and all our friendship is forgot.

   Clare. Her jealousy.

   Godfrida [*with an impatient gesture returns to her*
      book. After a brief pause]. Clare, did you ever
      make

A philtre of a wryneck smoked and ground ?

   Clare. That have I.

   Godfrida.   Did the philtre work your will ?

   Clare. She whom I made it for obtained her wish.

   Godfrida. Let us make such a love-compelling charm.

   Clare. There's art more subtle, magic braver far,

And craft more potent than a shelf of books.

No spell, no philtre, no melodious charm

Did ever make a hateful woman loved,

Or make her lovely. Beauty, youth, and grace

Enchant against the strongest sorcery.

   Godfrida. But that's no news ; for five strange years
      have men

Blushing or bronzed, or silvered, at my feet

Or at my window, said and sung such things.

Now, tell me of the philtre that you made.

Was it most mighty ?

   Clare.   It had no more might

Than any other beakerful of wine.

Godfrida. What wrought the purpose of the giver
 then ?

Clare. The purpose of the giver —

Godfrida [*with sudden conviction*]. Wrought itself !
When love has wrenched and broken all their pride,
Then luckless ladies turn to sorcery ;
But win their will by virtue of their will,
And not by means of thrice-decocted draughts.
The fixed resolve to wed the men they love,
Despite their soul's perdition, leads them on
To woo so sweetly and so valiantly,
That what their happier beauty could not do,
The beauty of despair accomplishes.
Philtres and charms, indeed ! My own desire
Enchants my soul, and shall enchant the soul
Of him whom I delight in and adore.

   Clare. Siward.

   Godfrida.   Yes, Siward. Oh ! I love him, Clare.
     [*Kneels at* CLARE'S *side, and lays her head in her*
      lap.]
What must I do, Clare ? Shall I send him word?

   Clare. I think you must not send him word.

   Godfrida.   Why, Clare ?
Ladies in straits like me have broken rules,
And won true husbands ; who have worshipped them

Because they had the courage of their love.

You think me foolish?

   Clare.   Only rash, sweetheart.

   Godfrida. And I think brave. I would be always

      brave.

Wise? Yes; but not with guile; and always brave.

Siward is brave.

   Clare.   Patience a little! Soon

Your purpose, as you said, may work itself

In some delightful, unexpected way.

   Godfrida. You think so, Clare?

      [*A knock is heard at the door on the left.* CLARE

         goes to the door. GODFRIDA *sits at the wheel.*

   Clare [*at the door*]. Who's there?

   Anselm [*off stage*].   I, Anselm.

   Godfrida [*whispering*].   No!

   Clare [*opening door*]. Godfrida is engaged.

   Anselm.   Tell her I know

The issue of the tournament.

   Godfrida [*whispering eagerly*]. Yes, yes!

      [CLARE *admits* ANSELM. *He is a tall, handsome*

        boy in his sixteenth year.]

Well, saucy boy, truant again?

   Anselm.   Oh, no!

I was forbidden to attend the lists.

Godfrida.　For what new mischief, sir ? —　But tell
　　me, now ;
Have you determined yet to run away,
And be a viking bold and scour the seas ?

　　　　　　　　　　[ANSELM *hangs his head.*]

What, Anselm, — sulky .　Not a kiss for me ?
Indeed, it 's time that ended.　I protest —
Look, Clare !　His upper lip !　But yesterday
Smoother than mine : and now, behold !

　　　　　[ANSELM *runs to* GODFRIDA *and kisses her cheek.*]

　　　　　　　　　　　　　　Young man,
You must be muzzled.

Anselm.　　　　　　　With a helmet !　Yes !
Next year I 'm going with Siward to the wars.
Godfrida, I have grown an inch since Christmas.

Godfrida.　You 'll be a giant, Anselm.

Anselm.　　　　　　　　　　Do you know
I measure round the chest almost as much
As Siward ?　Yes, and I can swing his sword.

Godfrida.　You 'll match him some day, Anselm, never
　　fear.

Anselm.　But do you think so ?　Would it not be
　　great
If I, unknown, could meet and conquer him,
And then, unhelmed, beg pardon on my knees ?

And yet I should not like to conquer him:
He never has been conquered.

 Godfrida.   Has he not?
This tournament may bring about a change.
I think you said you had some news of that.
I think he said so, Clare?

 Anselm.   I said so; yes,
Wishing to enter here.

 Godfrida.   You lied to me!
Begone!

 Anselm. Well —

 Godfrida.   Go!

 Anselm.   But I can truly tell
The issue of the tournament.   I can!
You know, they fight in companies to-day —
A score against a score with naked steel:
And Siward said — you mustn't say I told —
He meant to win the ribbon from your knight.

 Godfrida. From Adomar!   What did he know of
  that?
You mean to say you talk to him of me?

 Anselm. To you of him; of him, to you; what else?
Ah!   But he knew, as everybody knew,
Who wore your favour.   So he challenged him:
And Adomar turned white, but took the gage.

Siward will wear your favour now.   Some day
Perhaps I shall.

    Godfrida.   You foolish little boy!

    Anselm. You know you promised me to be my wife.

    Godfrida. I know.   I was your sweetheart; you were
        ten,

And I was fifteen.   You are fifteen now —
And tall and strong and handsome as a man.

    Anselm. Oh, damn!   Boy, man; man, boy!   God-
        frida, which?

    Godfrida [*laughing*].   Not man enough to storm
        becomingly.

                [ANSELM *is about to go in a huff.*]

Going already?   Come and say good-bye.
Come; kiss me, Anselm.   Will you not?   Well, then;

           [*She goes to* ANSELM *and kisses him.*]

This is the last time I shall kiss you, boy.
There, sir, and there!   Henceforth you are a man.
Good-bye, good-bye!

    Anselm.   No! keep me boy forever!

    Godfrida. I would I could!

    Anselm.   Your little sweetheart!

    Godfrida.   No,

Next year you 'll be a gallant cavalier,
And have a little sweetheart of your own.

Go; be a man.   [ANSELM *goes out sadly.*]
         A flower has withered, Clare.
                           [*Goes out at the back.*]

Re-enter ANSELM *triumphantly, followed by* SIWARD.
   SIWARD *is twenty-seven; strong, handsome face;*
   yellow hair; long Norseman's moustache. He wears
   a complete suit of tilting armour, with his visor
   raised. He has a crimson ribbon in his hand.

Anselm. Siward is come, victorious.
                           [*Looks about for* GODFRIDA.
Clare.   In the garden.
Siward [*laying his hand on* ANSELM'S *shoulder*].
My horse is at the door, dappled with froth,
Will you be kind to me, and ride him home?
Give him a pint of wine and see him groomed.
   Anselm. Ride Siward's horse?
                  [*Flings up his cap, and goes out joyfully.*
Siward.   Say not that I am come;
But say a messenger from Siward.
   Clare.   Why?
Siward. We have not met; but I would know her face,
And see none other in a chosen throng
Of the world's beauties: if her eyes greet me
As certainly my errand is half done.

Clare. I 'll say a messenger from Siward, sir.

[Goes out at the back.

SIWARD *removes his gauntlets, unbuckles his sword, and lays them on the table. Re-enter* GODFRIDA, *carrying roses. She leans against the garden-door in her surprise at beholding* SIWARD. SIWARD *does not see her entrance.*

Godfrida [to herself]. Siward himself!

[*Comes down stage.* SIWARD *approaches* GODFRIDA *eagerly.*] From Siward! Is he well?

Siward. Never so happy in his life before.

By me he sends Godfrida deference,

And something that was hers and now is hers

Again. [*Offers the ribbon.* GODFRIDA *lays her roses on the table, but does not take the ribbon.*

Godfrida. And how did Siward come by that?

Siward. Clusters and throngs of eyes massed up to heaven

Girt the loud tournament; but Siward watched

This only, streaming like a crimson flame

Above the *mêlée* on a lofty crest.

He spurred through drifts of dust and blood-stained plumes:

Three knights who barred the way he overthrew

With one unsplintered lance: then Adomar —

A foolish knight, but strong and deft in arms —
Fell at his touch like one by lightning struck.

   Godfrida. And is he killed?

   Siward.   No; Siward spared his life;
I have his ransom here.   But if you wish
He shall be killed?

   Godfrida.   Oh, God forbid!

   Siward.   Nay, then,
This Siward was a fool to waste his strength.
Farewell.   He shall return to Adomar
The favour which it seems was rightly his.

   Godfrida. You — you are Siward.   You — have come
       to me!

       [SIWARD *takes her hand; gradually draws her*
           into his embrace, and bends down to kiss her.]
Nay, let me go, sir.

   Siward.   To Sir Adomar?

   Godfrida. How can you say it!

        [*Takes the ribbon and ties it on his arm.*]
                 In the sight of men
Wear this and guard it, if in heaven's sight
You mean to wear my love about your heart.

   Siward. About my heart!   Accoutred in your love
Shall I not move unsmirched through courts: through
      war

Unwounded ; and through fire and flood unscathed.

> [*He embraces her; but she turns her face away
> when he would kiss her.*]

Must I not kiss you ?   Ah ! you love me not !

Godfrida.   I love you so, that were your ease concerned
I think I could compel my love to die.
But do not kiss me yet, Siward; not yet.

> [*They sit on the couch.   She helps him to remove
> his helmet.*]

And you are Siward !   Let me see you, close.
Is it not strange ? — most strange !   But yesterday
You were a being of another sphere,
Beyond my hail and seldom seen by me;
And now you are my hero in my arms.

Siward.   When shall I kiss you ?

Godfrida.   When the time has come.
A kiss of love is the most hallowed thing
That women have to give.   I pray you wait.
Our first kiss must be sweet and wonderful ;
And we must wear it like a talisman
Upon our lips, and in our memories
Enshrine and seal it everlastingly.

Siward.   Nay, all our kisses, though their number be
More than the flowers, more than the stars, shall live
Forever singly in our thoughts, each one

Denoted by its character, but all
Most fragrant, radiant, rich, and sacro-sanct.

Godfrida. All sacro-sanct! And I shall whisper,
    " Now," —
Nay, you shall know without a murmured word
When we must kiss. What — what if I should die
At the first kiss of love?

Siward.   Death might seal up
Our kiss more certainly than life : the grave
Is the securest casket.

Godfrida.   Death — of death
We talk, now that our lives begin to be
Of worth!

Siward.   For everything receives from love
Glory and virtue, grace and dignity
Before unknown; and chiefly shapeless death
Becomes most debonair and beautiful.

Godfrida. How great and how courageous is the world
That has within it such a quenchless fount
Of beauty and delight for all to drink !

Siward. Do you remember when our thirsty eyes
Partook their eager, earliest draught of love?

Godfrida. You rode bareheaded from your victory :
The happy people shouted " Siward ! "

Siward.   Yes !

3

And I looked up and at a lattice saw
Your face! [GODFRIDA *closes her eyes and he kisses her.*]
         Our second kiss!   Our souls first kissed
When first our glances blended.
[*Enter* THANGBRAND *hurriedly. About thirty-five;
     with a rough likeness to* SIWARD.]
     [*Starting up.*] Thangbrand!

Thangbrand. The Duchess bade me find you. She expects you now.

Godfrida [*has risen*]. The Duchess!

Thangbrand. She is not one that puts off till to-morrow. When Sir Siward left the lists she flung down her baton and despatched me for my master and the Seneschal for you, madam.

Godfrida. For me!

Thangbrand. He is close behind me. — Shall I wait on you at home, sir?

Siward. Surely. I must doff my harness before I go to court.

Thangbrand [*at the door*]. Here is master Gaucelm, sir.   [*Goes out.*

Enter GAUCELM, *passing Thangbrand at the door.
About fifty, wearing a chain of office.*

Gaucelm [*to* GODFRIDA]. The Duchess commands your attendance at the palace.

Godfrida. The Duchess shall be obeyed. At what time?

Gaucelm. Within an hour.

> [GODFRIDA *assents.* GAUCELM *goes out.*

Siward. The Duchess has some pique against you.

Godfrida.   Yes.

She is jealous of me, Siward; jealous — jealous !

Siward. Jealous of you ?

Godfrida.   She loves you, Siward.

Siward.   Me !

She only loves her country and herself.

Godfrida. How could she fail to love her warrior !

Siward, if she should offer you her hand ?

Siward. She will not.

Godfrida.   If she did, what would you do ?

Siward. I should reject it.

Godfrida.   Are you sure of that ?

We gather violets because the skies

Are far beyond our reach ; but if a star

Came down to us with sweet fire overbrimmed,

We might forget the simple violets.

Siward. And when the moon comes we forget the stars.

No other planet in the firmament

Can make my heart leap since your love-lit eyes

Looked on me from your lattice earnestly,

And all the aimless longing of my life

Began to flow in one full tide to you.

> [*He embraces her and goes out by the door on the left.*

GODFRIDA *walks across the stage slowly. Re-enter*
 ISEMBERT *unseen by* GODFRIDA. *He goes up*
 the stage and watches her. GODFRIDA, *crossing*
 again, takes a rose from the table.

Godfrida [*to herself*]. And all the aimless longing of
 my life
Began to flow in one full tide to you !

 Isembert [*comes down quickly*]. I passed your flashy
 ruffian at the door !
Are you Godfrida — or a serving-maid,
Whose heart goes pit-a-pat to hear a drum ?
Siward ! — a ruthless, wanton vagabond
Who puts his sword to auction — and his love !
What ! do you keep him, then ? — I heard them join
Your name with Siward's — as I hear the wind
That whispers naught for me. Could I believe
She who had known the treasure of my soul
In jewelled speech and silences that set
The thought to music, would degrade her heart
For a mere daub and signboard of a man —
A common fighting bully with a lie
In every word, a wench in every street !

 Godfrida. I cannot pardon this that you have said
Against my lover, though upon your face
Prone in the dust, you begged me all your life.

Isembert. Prone in the dust !— And so I broach your
    hate :
It shall have cause to flow, I promise you !

> [GODFRIDA *with a contemptuous look turns to go.*
>   ISEMBERT *seizes her hand, and the rose falls*
>   *at her feet.*]

I have more to say.   I came this time to plead —
I, who exalt myself above mankind,
Came meekly to implore a thing denied ;
For I forgave what I conceived to be
Perplexity at love's unlooked-for dawn.
Instead I find a sin against myself :
You knew me, and preferred a sort of slave,
A despicable huckster of his blood.
Now, though my senses still cry out for you,
I would not for a kingdom have your love.
But I shall make you mine in hate — a bond
Most intimate, most durable, most chaste.

> [*With a smothered scream* GODFRIDA *runs into the*
>   *garden.* ISEMBERT *crosses to go out. Look-*
>   *ing about with his hand on the door, he sees*
>   *the flower that fell from* GODFRIDA'S *hand ;*
>   *goes quickly and picks it up — stealthily, as if*
>   *ashamed to find himself doing so.*

ACT II.

SCENE. — *A lawn in the palace gardens. On the right
at the back, an arbour, open to the stage, overgrown
with roses. Through the trees on the left terraces are
seen ascending towards the palace, a wing of which
is visible in the distance. Towards the front the
ground rises on the left and is crested with shrubbery.
On the right near the front is an ornamental porch
overgrown with ivy; above it a grotto. At the
back and on both sides tall trees, shrubs, and flowers.
There are entrances at the back and on the right.*

When the curtain rises ERMENGARDE *is seated in
the arbour. She is about twenty-three; handsome,
restless. On the ground near her lies* SCIPIO, *a negro
page; beside him a lap-dog on a cushion. Courtiers
and Maids-of-honour, among whom is* CYNTHIA, *with
a lute, are grouped on the slope on the left.* GAUCELM
and attendants stand on the right. CYNTHIA'S *song
is begun before the curtain rises. During the first
verse* ERMENGARDE *rises and looks out at the back,
then stands just within the arbour. Music is con-*

*tinuous to the end of the song, the dialogue taking place
during the symphony between the verses.*

Cynthia [*singing*].

       Is it worth the learning
        This love they bless —
       Pale lovers yearning
        For happiness?
       Why do they glory in the night?
       What dream is theirs of proud delight?
        Is it worth the learning?

CYPRIAN *enters at the back before the close of the verse,
and goes at once to* ERMENGARDE, *who takes a step
towards him.*

Ermengarde.   Where is the Chancellor, Cyprian?
Cyprian.   At home, your Grace,
Absorbed in business of the state.
Ermengarde.   The state!
    [*Withdraws into the arbour impatiently, while*
       CYPRIAN *comes down and stands beside*
       GAUCELM.
Cynthia [*singing*].
       My heart is burning;
        It cries to me.

> Is it worth the learning
> What this may be?
> Why do I walk alone all day?
> " She is in love," the maidens say.
> Is love worth learning?

At the close of the second verse ISEMBERT *enters at the back quickly.* ERMENGARDE *meets him.*

Ermengarde. My lord, we have waited for you here!

Isembert. While I
Have wrought for you.

Ermengarde. You never want excuse.

Isembert. I am chiefly sorry that I cannot stretch
The minutes into hours to serve your Grace
With vigilance and effort sixty-fold.

> [ERMENGARDE *goes into the arbour.* ISEMBERT
> *follows her. During the song they are seen to
> converse,* ERMENGARDE *haughtily at first,
> then with her eyes bent on the ground;* ISEM-
> BERT, *surprised, appears to expostulate.*

Cynthia [*singing*].

> Was it worth the learning?
> He kissed my hand!
> Is love worth learning?
> I understand,

Though love may come and love may go,
It is the only thing to know :
Love's worth the learning.   •

Ermengarde [*leaving the arbour*]. Thanks for your
music. [Courtiers, *etc. rise.* ERMENGARDE *is
about to go out by the right, when* ISEMBERT
intercepts her]. I shall see them here;
But not together; Siward first, and then
Godfrida. When he comes send word to me.
I am wearied out; so sick with hope and fear
That like one poisoned I must walk, or faint.
                    [*Tries unsuccessfully to evade* ISEMBERT.
Isembert. Your Grace intends to marry Siward?
Ermengarde.   Yes.
Isembert. And to propose it bluntly to himself?
Ermengarde. And to propose it frankly to himself.
Isembert. If you would prosper, madam, give me
    leave
To mould a matter so momentous.
Ermengarde.   No!
In this I take my heart's advice alone.
I know I venture on an enterprise
Most hazardous; but which I may not shirk,
Because it leads me forward to myself —

A truer, greater self that waits beyond.

> [*She goes to* SCIPIO *and fondles the lap-dog; then looks about suddenly.*]

But where is Anselm, Scipio?

Scipio. Runaway!

Ermengarde. Why, Gaucelm, do you suffer these affronts?

The boy defies you : rule him better, sir.

> [*To the* Maids-of-honour.] March on before us — singing as you go.

> [CYNTHIA *resumes her song, and all except* ISEMBERT *and* CYPRIAN *go out by the right. The song is heard dying away in the distance.*]

Isembert. Did you observe the Duchess, Cyprian?

Cyprian. I never saw her so unlike herself.

Isembert. What do you think distracts her?

Cyprian. I should say,

But for her fixed resolve to die unwed,

That she had fallen in love.

Isembert. And so she has —

With Siward : crude instinctive savages

Love makes of women !

Cyprian. And of men, my lord.

Isembert. Mere males and females, Cyprian : that is all

The power of love can do. — I wish to write.

> [CYPRIAN *gives him materials, and he writes and*
> *folds a letter, talking the while.*]

A crowing fellow with a fair moustache
Struts up the street, and the whole hen-house clucks
With passion! — I am ousted, pecked away;
The Duchess undertakes her own affairs!
Well, other palates shall be scarified
By this same feast of thistles spread for mine.

> [*Gives the letter to* CYPRIAN.]

To Ludovic, at once.   Her Grace commands
Her army to be ready for the field
Upon a sudden call; and darkly hint —
This I have left unwritten — it may chance
That he shall lead. — Send Adomar to me;
He waits an audience: since the stalwart fool
Is mixed in this, we must get rid of him;
An ass may do more adventitious ill
Than twenty tigers. — Then search Berthold out,
And probe the heart of that conspiracy.:
Perhaps I may require it for myself.

> [CYPRIAN *goes out at the back.*]

I have a choice to make. [*Sits in arbour.*]   Should
    Ermengarde
Marry the Norseman, and my head escape

The axe, I sink into oblivion;
Or under Siward's thumb abide the turn
Of fortune's wheel; but if Godfrida wins
The ruffian, my dominion is renewed,
For in the shipwreck of her hopes, her Grace
Must cling to me. Thus either accident
Would test my fibre, twist and stretch my soul
Upon the rack of his or her delight
Whom most I hate! [*Rises.*] By my intelligence
I swear that neither love-sick simpleton
Shall marry Siward! By my wit, my will,
His golden locks and he have had their day!

[*Enter* ADOMAR *at the back. He is strongly built;
    stupid; anxious to be thought well of by himself and
    others.*]

[*Gaily.*] Well, Adomar, in what can I befriend you?
  Adomar. I wished to see you, Isembert. You
      know —
Perhaps you saw my overthrow to-day.
  Isembert. I heard of it.
  Adomar.   It was an accident.
Now, will you tell the Duchess how it chanced?
  Isembert. Tell her yourself.
  Adomar.   But if it came from you —

Re-enter GAUCELM *by the right.*

Gaucelm. Her Grace would know if Siward has arrived.

Isembert. Not yet. Assure her Grace that she shall
hear

The moment of his coming.

[GAUCELM *goes out.*]

Now, confess,

That Siward is the better man.

Adomar.   Perhaps;

I care not.

Isembert. No; why should you?

Adomar.   Every man

Must some day meet his master.

Isembert.   Yet no man

Is master every day.

Adomar.   Nor in all things!

He dances badly.

Isembert.   A barbarian!

Adomar. I scarcely was prepared : he rode me down

Before my beast had gained his tilting speed.

Isembert. I doubt it not.

Adomar.   And for the ribbon — well;

Let Siward keep it. What? a rag of silk!

Isembert. Let Siward flaunt it!

Adomar.   Till I win it back
In the next tourney.   I shall challenge him:
He took me at a disadvantage.

Isembert.   Nay,
Siward must wed Godfrida.

Adomar [*in much amazement*].   Must he!   Why?

Isembert.   And promptly, too, unless we want a duke.

              Re-enter GAUCELM *very hurriedly.*

Gaucelm.   Her Grace is most impatient.

Isembert.   So am I!
I shall myself announce him when he comes.

                        [GAUCELM *goes out reluctantly.*

Adomar [*importantly*].   Tell me of this.

Isembert.   Our haughty Ermengarde
Is torn with passion for the Norseman.

Adomar.   No!

Isembert.   And bent on marriage.

Adomar.   But it must not be.
We will not have the Norseman on our necks.
Let Siward wed Godfrida — now — to-day!

Isembert.   Most bravely counselled!   Ah! how strong
        is he
Who holds his heart subjected to his will!

Adomar.   I never loved her much.   It is a wrench;
But — is she not too slight for me?

Isembert.   By far!

Besides, the state demands the sacrifice.

Adomar. A man must pocket up his heart sometimes
When duty calls.

Isembert.   Now that I think of it,
I know how you may make the world forget
Your overthrow.

Adomar.   Oh! tell me, Isembert.

Isembert. Ride to Theodoric's tower and bring us word
If Count Esplandian approaches Arles.

Adomar. The Count Esplandian in Provence again!

Isembert. Go quickly; be the earliest with the news.

Adomar. Returning, breathless, tired, and travel-
      stained —

My horse, perhaps, dead at the palace-door —
I shall be famous, envied!

Isembert.   That you shall!

Adomar. I go then.   Not a word to any one! —
Why do you look so strangely, Isembert?

Isembert. I think of Solomon's own vanity
When he declared that all is vanity.

Adomar. What is the wisdom of it, Isembert?

Isembert.   That even the very grossest fools exist
Not all in vain, because once in their lives
They are made to serve some wise man's exigence,

If it were only by being easily
Kept out of the way.

Adomar.   Ha! Siward! Yes, I see.
We 'll keep him in the dark! — eh, Isembert?
He 'll hang his head when I come riding in!
A fop, a Norse adventurer! You know
My lance slipped, and he caught me by a fluke
Right on the vizor: children could upset
Giants with such a stroke.

Isembert.   I am sure of it.
Inform me, first of all, when you return.

Adomar. I will, and thank you kindly, Isembert.

> *[Goes out by the right.*
> *Enter* Attendant *at the back.*

Isembert. Is Siward there?

Attendant.   My lord, he has just arrived.

Isembert. Send him this way.

> *[Re-enter* ERMENGARDE *from the right.]*

Siward has come, your Grace.

Ermengarde. I wonder . . . Yes. Be near, most
faithful friend.

> *[*ISEMBERT *goes out by the right.*

[Enter SIWARD *at the back.* ERMENGARDE *receives him graciously.* SIWARD, *in a courtier's dress, is wearing* GODFRIDA'S *ribbon.]*

[*Harshly.*]   What 's that ?

Siward.   A pledge of love.

Ermengarde.   I know ; but whose ?

Siward.   Madam, my own.

Ermengarde [*furious*].   Who gave it to you, sir ?

Siward.   Godfrida, madam.

Ermengarde [*sinks down on the seat*].   Ah !

  [*Controlling herself, she rises and comes close to*

   SIWARD.]   I knew, my friend,

Your fancy to Godfrida turned : my page,

The truant, Anselm, all unconsciously,

Revealed the secret, gossiping : and she

Is fair and wise, and worth a warrior's love —

If there were none more fair, none worthier.

 Siward.   I will not understand you.

 Ermengarde.   But you do !

When post-haste from the tournament you rode —

Discourteously : [SIWARD *dissents.*] it was indeed a

  fault,

Most heinous in the office that you hold ! —

I guessed your errand, sir.   Did Adomar

Give up the ribbon for his life ?

 Siward.   He did.

 Ermengarde.   In that you scarce were chivalrous, I

  think.

Siward. Madam, you wrong yourself to blame me thus:
We fought *à outrance;* and Sir Adomar
Had taken up my challenge.   What of this?
The petty laws of silken marshal's men
Are fit for those who heed them.   For myself
I serve the state, and the state's noble head;
But live in my own world, a Norseman free.
To win my true love's gage I fought to-day,
And having won it left the mimic war.

    Ermengarde.   I take them back: the Duchess Ermen-
       garde
Withdraws her words! [*Returns to the arbour.*]   I would
      not hurt a hair
Upon your head — not one bright hair; and lo,
I wound the very marrow of your pride!
But, Norseman, Norseman, these are southern shores
Where ladies carry lightning in their veins.
How can I say that which I mean to say,
That which I must say?

    Siward.   You have said it, madam.
And I, your Grace's servant, honour you
With a more poignant reverence, knowing now
Your high heart's tender secret.   All my days
Await you like an escort cloaked in night.
My thoughts, my study of the storied world,

My courage and my skill in peace and war,

Are yours as long as they are mine to spend.

My love Godfrida has.

> [*During the following* SIWARD *gradually turns
> his face away from* ERMENGARDE.

Ermengarde.   It must be mine!

A hated wooer sought me: when you came

And whipped him off, I looked for you to ask

The recompense they said you sought, my hand.

> [*Pauses, expecting him to speak.*]

Your lofty spirit marks you out my mate:

My rank empowers and sanctions every way

The course I take in offering my crown,

My duchy and myself to one most wise,

Most noble, valiant, generous, and true.

> [*Sinks into the seat, trembling.*]

At first your silence hurt me: now I feel

How beautiful it is.

Siward.   My silence —

Re-enter Attendant *at the back.* ERMENGARDE *rises
relieved by the interruption.*

Ermengarde [*to* Attendant].   Well?

Attendant. Godfrida, madam.

Ermengarde. Wait. —[*To* SIWARD.] I shall demand

Your spoken answer later.   Leave me now:

Go to your house : consider all your life ;
Think of my love. ⠀To-morrow you shall speak.

⠀⠀⠀⠀⠀⠀⠀⠀[SIWARD *goes out by the back.*]

Ask my lord Chancellor to come to me.

⠀⠀⠀⠀[*She points the way and the* Attendant *goes out by
⠀⠀⠀⠀the right.*]

He dare not fling my offer in my face.

⠀⠀⠀⠀⠀⠀[*Re-enter* ISEMBERT *from the right.*]

I have over-rated, overtaxed my strength.

It is more arduous, more terrible

Than I imagined in my weakest hours.

⠀⠀*Isembert.* What, madam ?

⠀⠀*Ermengarde.* ⠀⠀⠀⠀⠀⠀⠀⠀⠀To confront a hostile will.

I trusted — must we always trust our hopes ? —

That like a goddess I should graciously

Descend and make a home in Siward's love.

I found it closed : it is inhabited :

A face looked out upon me from his heart.

⠀⠀*Isembert.* How did you deal with him ?

⠀⠀*Ermengarde.* ⠀⠀⠀⠀⠀⠀⠀⠀⠀⠀I lost myself !

He wore Godfrida's ribbon ; and I stormed

And chid him as a nurse would rate a child :

I felt him scorning me. ⠀What shall I do?

⠀⠀*Isembert.* Godfrida comes?

⠀⠀*Ermengarde.* ⠀⠀⠀⠀⠀⠀⠀⠀She is waiting.

Isembert.   See her now
Announce your marriage with the Constable,
And tell her since the gossip of the court
Has linked their names, she must at once declare
In public that the rumour is untrue.
   Ermengarde. But if she loves him that will break her
      heart !
   Isembert. Will yours be mended if she marries
      Siward ?
Amaze her, daunt her : in her fresh alarm
I 'll overpower her with a crowd — to-day
The city is your guest — and suddenly
Requiring her denial, so confound
Her judgment, that she shall comply
Outright with our demand.
   Ermengarde.   And afterwards?
   Isembert. Why, she will hang herself, or die of grief;
For courage is her idol. Siward then,
Hurt by Godfrida's fickleness and urged
By new ambition and the popular voice,
Will gladly marry you.
   Ermengarde.   But if her strength
Should not desert her ?
   Isembert.   But it shall ! The crowd,
By my instruction deeply overjoyed

At your betrothal, shall appear her foe ;
Alone, without a friend, against your will,
Against your people's will, her heart must break !

    Ermengarde. Already I 've been overharsh with
        her :
Why need *we* break her heart? Live and let live,
As kindly people say.

    Isembert.   Kill or be killed
As people calmly do. [*Watching her keenly.*] I 'll send
        your guard ;
And after bring your guests. [ERMENGARDE *dissents.*]
        How did you mean
To treat Godfrida ?

    Ermengarde.   Oh ! I cannot tell.

    Isembert. Madam, you must not flinch. With my
        advice
This glaring crisis never should have been :
But as the world must know what you have done —
So openly, so wilfully ! — proceed
High-handed to the issue ; or forbear —
That fools may flay your vanity, and make
Your heart a butt for shafts of ridicule !

        [ERMENGARDE *goes up stage distractedly, and*
           ISEMBERT *goes·out at the back, returning*
           almost immediately with GODFRIDA.]

[*To* GODFRIDA]. Mine you begin to be, love
— mine, in hate.

　　　　　　　　　　[*Goes out at the back.*

[GODFRIDA *is much agitated and looks wistfully
at* ERMENGARDE, *who regards her coldly.*

Ermengarde. Did Siward pass you?

Godfrida [*recovering self-possession*]. Yes; I spoke
to him.

Ermengarde [*comes close to* GODFRIDA *and speaks at
her ear*]. You shall not have the Norseman: he
is mine.

You shall renounce him publicly to-day:
I sent for him and told him all my love:
We shall be married soon.

　　Godfrida [*proudly*].　　He came to me.

Ermengarde. While I must send! How dare you!
　　. . . So I did,

Godfrida! Yes, and be you warned by that.
I am neither cruel nor tyrannical;
But I must wed this gentle god of war;
Nothing shall stay me: I have sent a spy
Into the darkest corners of my soul,
And find no enemy within myself
Powerful enough to combat my desire.

　　Godfrida. Siward will marry me.

Ermengarde.   That shall he not!
And when I ask you, now, before the court
You shall declare you never loved him.

   Godfrida.   I!
I will not!

   Ermengarde. But you shall! by heaven, you shall!

   Godfrida. By Siward's love for me, by mine for him —

   Ermengarde. You shall!

   Godfrida.   No! I shall not!

   Ermengarde.   No enemy
Is half so fatal as a friend estranged.
I am jealous of you! Do my will, or dread
My vengeance. I have pledged myself: he knows,
And now you know, my passion and my purpose,
And none shall thwart or scorn me. You, indeed!

   Godfrida [*with malice*]. Permit me now to go; for
     Siward waits:
He said he would attend my coming forth.

   Ermengarde. I shall take care you meet him not
     again
Till you have given him up before the world.

     [GODFRIDA *bows disdainfully, and is about to go
       out, when she is met by the* Lieutenant *with
       the guard, who enter at the back, salute and
       form, blocking the way.* GODFRIDA *over-*

> *comes her amazement and turns defiantly on*
> ERMENGARDE.

Godfrida. Madam, although you were to bury me
Deep in a dungeon or an unknown grave,
Our happy love would not be desolate;
For on my mouth is Siward's kiss; on his
My kiss lies, an inviolable bond;
And you can never sever from my soul
The soul of Siward, mine in life, in death.

Ermengarde. Now friendship, pity, die indeed! To eat
Your words, to drink your tears, to swallow down
Your bursting heart before the court, and I
Seated triumphantly observing you!
Oh! you will find that worse than chains or death.

Re-enter ISEMBERT *with* Ladies *and* Gentlemen *at the
back.* ANSELM *enters last and leans against a tree,
disconsolately.* ISEMBERT *leads* GODFRIDA *up stage
and stations her on the left of* ERMENGARDE, *who
stands in front of the arbour.* ISEMBERT *then looks*
about anxiously and crosses to ANSELM. GAUCELM,
CYNTHIA, Courtiers *and* Maids-of-Honour *re-enter
from the right.*

Isembert [*to* ANSELM]. Is Siward here?

Anselm.   He is not coming.

Isembert.   Not?

Anselm. The Duchess sent him home.

Isembert.   Impossible!
A bungled message. Bid him come at once:
I saw you with him in the palace-hall.

  Anselm. I told him so! He 'll think me wiser now.

         [Goes out at the back.

   [ISEMBERT *goes up stage and stands on* ERMEN-
    GARDE'S *right. The crowd is mostly on the
    right, leaving the back entrance visible to the
    audience.*

Isembert. Upon her Grace's part I welcome you.
Your loyalty, your sympathy — your hearts
Our mistress needs; not as a ruler now,
But as a friend. — More burdensome it is
To wield authority than to obey.
If mighty kings, discerning sovereign power
To be dull torture, abdicate their thrones,
Or maddened by dominion, to themselves
Impute prerogatives of deity,
Some doom more evil still may overwhelm
A woman, set alone above the world.
Therefore her Grace determines to forsake
The lofty solitude wherein the hearts
Of monarchs grow unhuman, and to steep
Her life in the brave love and happy care

That wives and mothers know.

Voices.   God save her Grace!

Isembert. It was her earlier design to live
A maiden all her days, lest, marrying,
She should provoke that destiny untoward,
A ruthless master for herself and you —
Such as the Count Esplandian of Toulouse
Who thought to win her love with battering-rams.
But he who beat that stubborn warrior back —

Voices [astonished and pleased].   Siward!

Ermengarde [overjoyed].   You love him too?

Voices.   Yes, yes, your Grace;
Siward! A Siward!

Ermengarde.   Loyal, generous friends,
I thank you from my heart.

Voices.   God save your Grace!

> [GODFRIDA *shrinks back into the arbour.* ISEM-
> BERT, *passing behind* ERMENGARDE, *takes*
> GODFRIDA'S *hand and leads her forward.*

Ermengarde [to GODFRIDA]. Now is the time I spoke
of.

Isembert.   All her life
Her Grace's confidante shall be Provence;
Her people is her only bosom-friend:
And not one film of slander must obscure

Her happy marriage, fated to control
The tides of your contentment and of hers.
I understand a shapeless rumour walks
Haunting this lady's name : but she herself
Will lay the phantom now.

   Ermengarde.   Godfrida, speak
In all good faith, and let my people know
Siward was never anything to you.

     Godfrida [*recovers presence of mind. With all her*
        force]. She lies! The Duchess lies! Siward is
        mine !

       [ISEMBERT *is intensely surprised, and stares in ad-*
         miration at GODFRIDA. ERMENGARDE *with*
         a cry lifts her hand clenched to strike GOD-
         FRIDA, *when* SIWARD *enters with* ANSELM.

   Siward. Godfrida!

       [GODFRIDA *runs to* SIWARD *and falls into his*
        arms.

   Ermengarde [*sinks into the seat*]. Ah !

   Isembert [*in* ERMENGARDE'S *ear*].   Bid me dis-
     miss them, madam.

   Godfrida. I was afraid a moment — only one.

   Isembert. Bid me dismiss them, madam.

   Ermengarde.   No ; not yet.
[*To* SIWARD.] What brings you here ?

Siward.   The kindest destiny.

Ermengarde [*rises*]. But I forbade you, sir.

> [SIWARD *looks to* ANSELM; ANSELM *looks to* ISEM-
> BERT; ERMENGARDE *follows their glances.*

Isembert.   I sent for him.

Ermengarde [*looks wildly at* ISEMBERT, *then steps
forward and cries in a piercing voice*]. My people,
now I need your constant hearts!

Voices. God save your Grace!

Ermengarde.   Those whom I trusted most
Have covered me with shame before you all!
I am betrayed! Who is on my side — who?

Isembert [*drawing his sword*]. For Ermengarde!

All the Men [*with drawn swords*].   Provence
and Ermengarde!

Isembert. Madam, you are betrayed: look in your
heart,
And find the traitor there.

Ermengarde.   My heart, indeed!
It is too true to me! — Give up your sword!

Isembert [*yielding his sword to* ERMENGARDE]. Into
your hands.

Ermengarde.   And yours, Sir Constable.

Siward [*yielding his sword to the* Lieutenant]. Madam,
this is as guilty as its lord.

Ermengarde. These traitors I shall question privately!
But do not leave me, friends: it gives me strength
To think my people are within my house:
And when this pitiful, this childish plot
Is sifted, as it shall be instantly,
I may again take counsel with your hearts.

       [*Pointing to* SIWARD *and* GODFRIDA
Sever these two; and see you guard them well.

       [*Pointing to* ISEMBERT.
Lead him now to the hall.

Voices.   God save your Grace!

ACT-DROP.

ACT III.

SCENE. — *The Hall of the Palace. At the back to the left a high and broad doorway. Above the doorway is a gallery with a small window, and doors. On the right at the back a large window: on the extreme right, a small door surmounted by a cross. Down right is a large window, and below it, near the front, a door. On the left toward the front is a dais, on which a throne stands. Below the dais a door. The walls are hung with tapestry, and there is stained glass in all the windows. Lamps, conveniently. A few seats about the dais. It is sunset when the act opens. The moon rises about the middle of the act. Ermengarde is seated on one of the seats near the dais, and* ISEMBERT *is led in by the large door when the act-drop rises.*

Ermengarde. You are the head of this conspiracy?

Isembert. Madam, I know of no conspiracy.

Ermengarde. Why summon Siward then? The thing was schemed
To tame me to your power.

    Isembert.   Unjustly urged!

Ermengarde. " The Duchess lies ! " she said; "the
  Duchess lies ! "
Would even a crazy creature, in the power
Of arbitrary rivalship, alone,
And unabetted, helplessly invoke
Immortal enmity?   " The Duchess lies ! "
 Isembert.   Madam, your jealousy has blinded you.
 Ermengarde. You mean it has unsealed my eyes.
  Disclose
The secret of this treason!— Speak!— Confess!
Sir, there 's a spindle underground, the rack,
Famous for winding up conspiracies;
And I shall have you all three wrung at once
To scream against each other.
     [Goes out by the door on the left.
 Isembert.   Madam! [*To himself.*] Time
I must have now !   What shall I do?   Make love !
[*At the door.*]   Madam !
    Re-enter ERMENGARDE.
 Ermengarde.   One word : will you confess the truth ?
 Isembert. Question me : you shall judge.
 Ermengarde.   Why did you send
For Siward ?
 Isembert. That he might abhor your Grace,
Beholding your abuse of power.

Ermengarde [*amazed*].   But why?

Isembert. Because I would not have you marry
    him :

I would not have you marry any one.

I meet you every day : I touch your hand :

I see you in your most enthralling moods

Of informality and indolence :

I know your subtle brain, your fiery soul;

To me you are the very source of life.

    [ERMENGARDE *turns her face from him, unable to*
        hide her gratification. He relieves himself
        with a grimace.]

But were your gracious spirit coffined up

In wedlock, the devouring sepulchre

Of beauty, eminence, distinction, love —

Should you, who are the sun, become a lamp

For household uses, then the world would end

Here in Provence.   I beg you not to wed !

Ermengarde [*turns towards him*]. Poor Isembert! I
    understand you not ;

But feel a faithful passion in your words.

You must not thwart me further : I have none

To trust but you.

    Isembert.   Trust me, and I obey :

But when you bring me suddenly to work

Upon a secret purpose of your own,
No wonder I upset it.

  Ermengarde.   Yet, the doubt!—
Oh, sir, be true!— What gave Godfrida strength
To brave my power?

  Isembert.   Need a true lover ask?

  Ermengarde. But does she love like me?

  Isembert.   True lovers feel
As if their passion were original —
A virgin revelation to themselves
Alone imparted.

  Ermengarde. Would Godfrida die
Were I to marry Siward?

  Isembert.   If her love
Is absolute — perhaps.

  Ermengarde. My love is absolute:
My life is all transmuted into love:
Help me to save my life.   Show me the way
To wreak my vengeance on the sorceress
Who stole my Siward's heart.

  Isembert.   The sorceress?

  Ermengarde. Godfrida.   When our friendship held,
    we played
With philtres and enchantments, she and I;
But she has used her craft.

Isembert.   It must be so:

How else could any man of Siward's rank

Reject you and your throne?

    Ermengarde.   How else, indeed?

And I shall have her tried for sorcery.

Kill or be killed — your motto, Isembert:

Highhanded to the end!

    Isembert.   But warily;

The highest hand is that which works unseen.

Commit your happiness to me ; my love

Will bear the proof.

    Ermengarde.   What will you do?

    Isembert.   The best.

Events and passions blindly hurry by;

I touch them as they pass, deflecting them

Towards my aim.

    Ermengarde.   I give you leave.

    Isembert.   First then,

I see Godfrida here alone.

    Ermengarde.   Suppose —

Suppose that I see Siward here alone,

Beforehand!   Has it reached his brain, his heart,

What marriage with me means?   Not yet, I think;

But if in all my state I came to him,

And kneeling, laid my coronet at his feet ! —
I am inspired with this !

Isembert.   And being scorned
Your Grace would die of shame.

Ermengarde.   It is my life
I seek to purchase ; for without his love
I 'd scorn myself and be ashamed to live.

> [*Crosses to the left quickly.*

Isembert. I am a prisoner still.

Ermengarde.   Summon the guard.

> [ISEMBERT *brings in* Halberdiers *from the back,*
> *who promptly guard him.*]

Your charge is at an end.

> [Halberdiers *salute and go out.*]

                                Oh, now I know
That I shall win him.

Isembert.   And if not?

Ermengarde.   Why then
You shall proceed unfettered.   But this time
My heart is sure : he shall at last perceive
How strong, how passionate, how great I am !

> [*Goes out by the door on the left.*

Isembert.   This, now, is love — the desperate, jealous
        love
To anguish doomed; for no felicity
Can spring in men, except from barbèd roots

Of discontent and envy deeply struck
In some sore heart that hoped to have the flower.

> [*Goes out by the door on the right.*
> *Enter* GAUCELM *by the door on the left; and* Attendants *by the large door. They light the lamps. The moonlight begins to shine on the windows. The* Attendants *have gone out, and* GAUCELM *is about to go out, when* ANSELM *and* THANGBRAND *enter by the door on the right.*

Anselm. Gaucelm! Gaucelm! Can we see her Grace?

Gaucelm. Where have you been rambling all day, sir? I am amazed that you should have the foolhardiness to propose to come into her Grace's presence.

Anselm. But I am foolhardy, Gaucelm. Will you ask her Grace if Siward's man, Thangbrand, may wait upon him?

Gaucelm. I will, sir; and say something besides.

> [*Goes out by the door on the left.*

Anselm. He will now accuse me of insubordination. Well, never mind. We are in luck, Thangbrand. I can show you how Siward shall escape. [*Leads* THANGBRAND *to the small door at the back.*] Remember, you must be sure to say to him at once that it was my plan, Thangbrand. You will say it was my plan?

Thangbrand. Your plan, young master. Where is his cell?

Anselm. Oh, he is not in a cell! This chapel leads to the corridor upon which the room opens where Siward is imprisoned. A sentinel is on guard. As soon as you are admitted you must change habits with Siward. I shall come along the corridor as if by chance, and enter into conversation with the sentinel.

Thangbrand. Not if I were the sentinel.

Anselm. But you are not the sentinel. Then Siward must knock, and when the door is opened he steps out in your habit, and I say, "Ah, Thangbrand! How does Siward take his fall?"—or something like that—you see? When the sentinel peeps into the room before fastening the door again, he shall see only your back, for you must be looking out at the window in Siward's habit. Meanwhile Siward and I saunter up the corridor, and through the chapel to this gallery, from which a passage leads directly out of the palace.

Thangbrand. It may succeed; but not if I were the sentinel. — And what will they do with me, do you think?

Anselm. And with me? I would risk anything for Siward.

Thangbrand. And so would I !

Re-enter GAUCELM.

Gaucelm. The Duchess permits Thangbrand to visit his master.

Anselm. Splendid !

Gaucelm. The Duchess commands her disobedient page, Anselm, to wait upon her immediately.

Anselm. But —

Gaucelm. On pain of imprisonment.

Anselm. Oh! — You will wish you had held your tongue, master Seneschal. I shall tread upon your toes for this — upon every corn in your splay-footed vanity.

[*Goes out impatiently by the door on the left.* THANGBRAND *stares stolidly at* GAUCELM *and goes out by the door on the right.*

Enter INGLERAM *and* DAGOBERT *by the large door.*

Gaucelm. Good evening, Sir Ingleram. Good evening, sir.

Ingleram. What is this ridiculous story about my niece ?

Gaucelm. I think she hardly finds it ridiculous, sir.

Ingleram. It is true, then. She is in prison ?

Gaucelm. Her liberty is certainly restrained.

Ingleram. And Siward and Isembert ?

Gaucelm. They also are under guard.

Ingleram. On a charge of conspiracy ? [GAUCELM *assents.*] I pray you, say to the Duchess that I will become surety for my niece.

Dagobert. And I also, if her uncle is not sufficient.

Gaucelm. Frankly, gentlemen, I cannot promise. I carried a request to her Grace just before you came : she granted it, but she forbade me to trouble her again.

Dagobert. Entreat one of her ladies to carry it.

Gaucelm. I shall endeavour the utmost. Will you wait ?

Ingleram. I shall be much your debtor.

Dagobert. And I.

    [GAUCELM *goes out by the door on the left.*

Ingleram. Can we be suspected ?

Dagobert. I think not.

Enter CYPRIAN *and* BERTHOLD *by the large door.*
  BERTHOLD *has reached the grave and wise stage of intoxication.*

Cyprian. We saw you enter the palace and came after to know the news.

Ingleram. The news of what ?

Berthold. Any — news.

Ingleram. Your feet stumble and your tongue trips, sir.

Berthold. Policy — good policy.

Ingleram. Policy ! I call it drunkenness.

Berthold. The same thing. You can never be supposed conspirators so long as I frequent your company.

Keep a good heart: for I shall be continually drunk till Esplandian comes: that will obviate all suspicion.

Cyprian. Have you the message from Esplandian you spoke of in the morning?

Ingleram. Yes; but let me tell you, sir, I suspect you. You are Isembert's right-hand man. What do these sudden arrests mean?

Cyprian. How should I know? Some caprice of the Duchess's.

Dagobert. The Duchess's caprices have hitherto been dictated by Isembert.

Cyprian. He is himself a prisoner.

Dagobert. We are not to be blinded by that.

Cyprian. Umph! Can you not understand? Isembert bought me, and used me, taking my ignoble nature for granted. The conquest of Provence by Esplandian will ruin him: I shall see him reduced to ask alms of me. Show me the letter.

Ingleram. I shall come to you with it after my business here.

Cyprian. But this is an excellent rendezvous. In the hall of the palace, and accompanied by the politic Berthold, who shall suspect us? [INGLERAM *gives him a letter, which he reads.*] Ah! here is no stealthy whisper in an alcove, of less value than a lover's sigh! Stout parchment and black ink! Dagobert to be Constable; you to have Godfrida's estate; and lands and money for all your associates.

Ingleram. I call it a substantial promise.

Cyprian [*returns the letter*]. And a simple piece of villainy too. When the battle joins we are to kill Siward, and go over to Esplandian with all who will follow us.

Ingleram. That is his meaning.

Cyprian. He seems to be heartily afraid of Siward.

Ingleram. He knows Siward's quality by experience.

Berthold [*buttonholing* INGLERAM *with one hand and flourishing the other at* DAGOBERT]. Extraordinary men — men who interfere with the common course of events — should always be killed. We must kill Isembert, too.

Cyprian. Oh, no! we reserve him for a worse fate. Indigence to men like Isembert is more terrible than death.

Berthold. I would have him killed. He called me a bottle. Superior persons should be killed : to be superior is to have an unjust advantage over the rest of the world.

Cyprian. The whole philosophy of envy!— Come along, Berthold; you shall impart all your wisdom to me. —[*To* INGLERAM.] Shall I see you to-night?

Ingleram. Yes; at my house.

[CYPRIAN *and* BERTHOLD *go out by the large door.*
Re-enter GAUCELM *with* Halberdiers *by the*
door on the left.]

Well, Gaucelm?

Gaucelm.   As I feared ; none dared intrude.

But you must go.   She comes to question Siward.

[INGLERAM *attempts to take* GAUCELM *aside.*]

No; no!   I cannot listen. [*To the* Halberdiers]. Clear
the hall !

[INGLERAM *and* DAGOBERT *go out reluctantly by*
the large door, followed by the Halberdiers,
who form outside the door.   Then GAUCELM
ushers ERMENGARDE *by the door on the left.*
ANSELM *and* Maids-of-Honour *attend her.*
She is in her robes of state, and wears a ducal
crown.   She sits on one of the chairs near the
dais.   At a sign from her GAUCELM, AN-
SELM, *and* Maids-of-Honour *go out by the*
door on the left.   Then SIWARD *is brought*
in by the door on the right.]

Ermengarde.   Siward, I cannot, will not, give you up.

[SIWARD *makes an impatient gesture.*]

Indeed, there is none like you, Siward — none !

A crafty man would soon have groped his way

To my soul's inner room; your loyalty
Halted upon the threshold of my thought,
Nor cast a single curious glance within.
Until I spoke had you no hint, no glimpse
Of my consuming love? Did you not hear
Across the slumbering city, how my heart
Kept nightly vigil, beating "Siward, Siward"?

　　Siward. To me you were the symbol of the state
In whose defence I rose to eminence.
Release Godfrida; set me also free:
Then shall I think you love me.

　　Ermengarde.　　　　　　　Bitter!—rude!
Why do you love Godfrida?

　　Siward.　　　　　Why do you
Love me?

　　Ermengarde. Because you are the only man
In all the world to whom I would entrust
My body and my soul. — Godfrida's love?
A sweet and fair domestic comedy!
A toy—a paltry feather in your cap,
That in the tumult of a soldier's life
Must soon grow limp and drop into the mire.
My love, begirt with wars, with cares of state
Heavily jewelled, would fulfil and deck
Your span of years as richly as the night

Is belted, bossed, and overhung with stars :
Lo ! at your feet I and my passion lie !

> [*Kneels and lays her crown at* SIWARD'S *feet.   He
> lifts the crown, replaces it on her head, and
> leads her to a seat.*

Siward.   Godfrida has my love ; but I have done
With all reproach and censure, and will speak
Solicitously now, and heedfully
As mortals should when the strong wine of life
Maddens a suffering soul — humbly, indeed,
For I have drunken deep of the same cup. —
A landless wanderer, shackled to my sword,
I followed chance and peril, knowing love
But as a pastime, till a miracle
Befell me in your city.

Ermengarde [*under her breath*].   What!
Siward.   I rode
One evening from a field where victory
Had flattered me ; the doting multitude
Shouted my name ; my horse on garlands trod ;
I ceased to think, and yielded to the hour.
On my entranced and twilight mood there fell
Godfrida's eyes, still and devout with love.
Her spellbound brows shed from her lattice power
Upon my fancy and upon my will.

It seemed to me my life was rooted up
And set anew in virgin ground, whose strength
Brought forth a sudden passion as divine
As that which ripened in Godfrida's breast.
I love her and shall love her always.   None
Came ever fresher from on high than she.
Your Grace must suffer love to work its will.

   Ermengarde. I do!   I suffer — for your happiness.

   Siward. Our lives are tangled in a lover's knot,
Which may not be undone — except by you.

   Ermengarde. That would be by my death, then: I
     should die
If you were married to Godfrida — her
Who gave the lie to me!   Disgraced and scorned,
'T is I shall cut this knot — and this one too!

     [*She tries to snatch* GODFRIDA'S *ribbon from*
       SIWARD'S *arm. He grasps her wrists and*
       she screams.

   Siward. You might as well attempt to wrench the
     moon
From her deep home in heaven.   My heart is heaven,
For there Godfrida dwells.

  Re-enter ISEMBERT *hurriedly by the door on the right.*

  Ermengarde [*to* ISEMBERT].   Do what you will!
          [*Goes out by the door on the left.*

Siward. How comes it you are free?

Isembert.   Her Grace has found
My treachery peculiar diligence
In her behalf.

Siward.   Are you my enemy?

Isembert.   If you suspect me, then I must be so:
Fear makes an enemy of truth itself.

      [*Brings in* SIWARD'S Guard *by the door on the
        right.*

Siward. When I regain my freedom I shall ask
A clear account of your complicity
In these unworthy dealings.

Isembert.   Understand,
I answer my inferiors as I please.

Siward. And with my sword I punish insolence.

       [*Goes out, guarded, by the door on the right.*

Isembert. So!

     [*Re-enter* CYPRIAN *by the large door.*]

          Cyprian! The plot?

Cyprian.   An idle toy —
A bubble. If Esplandian wins, they hope
To profit in the scramble.

Isembert.   Shallow apes!

Cyprian. What must I say, my lord, if I am asked,
As I will be, concerning your arrest?

Isembert. Say I am free!— Go, now, and tell the
    guard
The Duchess waits to see Godfrida here.

    [CYPRIAN *goes out by the door on the right.*

Adomar [*off the stage*]. I must! I will! Stand back!

    [*Enter* ADOMAR *by the large door, booted, spurred,
        travel-stained, excited.*]

                      Esplandian comes!
I saw his outposts from Theodoric's tower.
Where is the Duchess?

                [*Crosses to left door.*

Isembert.   Adomar!
Adomar.   What now?
Isembert. You cannot see her.
Adomar.   Cannot see her?
Isembert.   No.

    [*Crosses to* ADOMAR *and leads him to the door at
      the back.*]

You love Godfrida? Well; strange things have chanced.
You must withhold these tidings for a while.

    Adomar. But, Isembert—
    Isembert.   Tell no one. Everything
Depends upon your silence.

    Adomar.   On the way

I passed another riding with the news:
He may forestall me if I speak not now.

   Isembert. A childish thought! For shame! Wait
    patiently!
I have a great surprise in store for you.

          [*Bundles* ADOMAR *out by the large door.*
   GODFRIDA *is ushered in by the door on the right.*

Godfrida. Where is the Duchess?

Isembert.   You are left to me.

Godfrida. To you!— Unquestioned — now — at once?

Isembert.   .   At once!
My vengeance never waits on providence.
I have devised a torture that shall last
Your time and mine : for you shall be my wife.

   Godfrida. Indeed? Two people would be tortured
    then.

   Isembert. A fiery furnace for us both! — To-day
Twice have I put your spirit to the test:
You shrank before the promise of my hate;
But in the grip of it your courage came:
So when I heard you say "The Duchess lies!"
You conquered me. And I must conquer you:
I will have victory.

   Godfrida.   I fear you not:
You are of those who follow ruthlessly

Their self-determined aims, who deem themselves
The governors of destiny; but let
Ingenuous natures their intrigues withstand,
Then these presumptuous overseers of fate,
Rebuked and quelled, are lost in impotence.

    Isembert. In impotence! Your liberty, your life —
I hold them in the hollow of my hand!

    Godfrida. I understood it was my love you sought.

                                  [*A pause.*

    Isembert. And hope to capture even yet. Your scorn
Bruising my heart, releases gentle thoughts
To help me at my need. — Is it my age
Repels you? Maiden, love for me is still
Wonder and adoration. Fresh as yours
My heart is, and as young. Ambition held
Me prisoner: when at last I burst its bonds
And reached the height of power, I found you there:
For on the day I grasped the seal you came
To wish me joy — the laughing girl I tossed
A word to sometimes, in a moment grown
A woman, far off, sweet and grave as night;
Deep mystery in her eyes, and starry chains
Of passion for my new-delivered soul.

    Godfrida. I did, indeed, admire you, Isembert;
But never dreamt of love.

Isembert.   I dreamt of it ;
And wooed you long.   Was I too haughty ?   Now
Let me make full amends.

> [*He kneels and takes her hand, which she with-
> draws.   He then grasps her skirt.*]

Oh ! I am sure
That Siward loves you not so tenderly
As I do ; and I think no soul of man
Did ever suffer pangs more merciless
Than mine, desiring you for my delight,
My mistress, and my wife.

Godfrida.   You shame yourself
To crawl so at my feet.

Isembert [*rises*].   What must I do ?
Be great, and tell me how to win your love!

Godfrida.   I am content to undergo the hate
You offered first.

Isembert.   But I am not content
To be the abject hateful thing that hates :
I have had a vision of the soul of life,
And love alone is worthy !

Godfrida.   Love alone !
Then you will pardon Siward's love and mine,
And envy not at our felicity ;
For love must pardon love — must pardon fate.

Isembert.   And who shall pardon me?   My life must
    shrink,
And all the strength and sweetness of my love
Decay to nourish your felicity —
Your sleek felicity!   Who shall forgive
My fate — my infelicity?   Reply!
   Godfrida.   Our wills are at a deadlock!
   Isembert.   Truly!   Death
May be the only pardoner for us! —
You choose my hate?
   Godfrida.   I choose my love!
   Isembert.   And make
Me mean and devilish!   To be the king
Of all the world, or of the noblest sphere
That space can boast, the masterpiece of time,
Would not console my infinite distress!
Not to be loved, loving you as I do! —
Oh, it is monstrous, horrible, unjust
That men should suffer thus! — You doom my soul,
Most capable of every lofty joy,
To fester in a slough of jealousy,
Of envy, malice, rancour!   Pitiless
As happy love itself my hate shall be!

      [GODFRIDA *stands in deep distress.* ISEMBERT
        brings in Ladies *and* Gentlemen, *the* Lieu-

tenant *with* Halberdiers *and* ADOMAR *by
the large door;* ERMENGARDE, GAUCELM,
ANSELM, *and* Maids-of-Honour *by the door
on the left. While the crowd is arranging
itself* ISEMBERT *and* ERMENGARDE *talk earnestly together, and ascend the steps of the
dais.*

Ermengarde.   Once more, Provence, I' need your
  loyalty:
My happiness is founded on your hearts.
You witnessed my betrayal: now behold
How swiftly justice follows treachery!

[Indicating ISEMBERT.]

For this most faithful friend, he erred through zeal
In my behalf; no blame is linked with him.
Sit, Isembert. 'T is you shall judge this cause,
Since I myself must testify against
The wanton sorceress who stole from me
What most on earth I prized.

Voices.   God save your Grace!

  [ISEMBERT *has a chair placed on the dais, and
    when* ERMENGARDE *is seated in it, he takes
    the throne.* ANSELM *stations himself at the
    door on the right;* GAUCELM *at that on the
    left.* Ladies *are seated in the chairs about*

*the dais. There is a clear space from the
front of the dais to the door on the right.
The rest of the stage is crowded.* GODFRIDA
*stands near the centre of the stage, well
towards the front. As soon as* ISEMBERT
begins to speak, ANSELM *slips out by the door
on the right.*

Isembert. Godfrida, you are charged with sorcery
Upon the accusation of her Grace.

Godfrida. With sorcery!—Indeed, her Grace knows
        well
The compass of my magic !

Isembert [*to* ERMENGARDE].   You were friends
At one time, madam.

Ermengarde.   Yes, and played at witchcraft
With amulets and charms and periapts,
Till she employed her art to work her will.

Isembert. How do you know she used her heathen
        power
On Siward's mind ?

Ermengarde.   By tokens manifold.
Is it not known to all that till to-day
Godfrida and the Norseman never met?
No word, no letter, not a syllable,
No message, gift, or sign between them passed :

And yet you saw how Siward galloped off
Like a rude bandit from the tournament
The moment her enchanted ribbon touched
His hand, gauntleted though it was.

    Isembert. This seems like witchcraft. Was there any
       reason
Why Siward should have spurned Godfrida's love
Had he been free from her resistless spell ?

    Ermengarde. There was : he might have won a nobler
       love.

    Isembert. What was the nature of Godfrida's charm ?

    Ermengarde. Siward himself in his delirious talk
Revealed the method of her sorcery.
In ambush at her window long she watched
Till fortune brought him riding past her lair.
Then over him she flung with silent spells
So searching and so terrible a look,
That she extorted from his inmost will
All power to change or choose, and made him hers
Until the charm be broken. Now he raves
Of miracles and of a flowering plant
That blossoms in his heart. Most sad it is
To see his noble spirit overcome
By such unhallowed means.

    Isembert.   How overcome ?

Save in his frenzied passion, I suppose
He has his wits and can command himself.

 Ermengarde. In everything but this.

 Isembert.   A fatal sign!
Godfrida, have you anything to say?

 Godfrida. Nothing to you, and nothing to her
  Grace;
For you are clearly leagued to ruin me:
But I appeal to every open mind.
Enchantments, necromancy, mysteries
Of numbers, and the wisdom of the stars
Her Grace and I together conned: we sought
Occult abilities in stones and herbs,
In earths and subtle creatures of the dark:
But innocently, with a child's delight
In things prohibited; or if the use
Of magic tempted us — as, I confess,
It tempted me at divers idle times —
We still resisted while our friendship held:
Nor have I yielded since.

 Ermengarde.   You dare to hint
That I —

 Godfrida. I dare do anything but lie;
For am I not contending for my love?
If there be any here who feel, who think,

Whose hearts say now, or who remember still
What love is, I beseech them to believe
That nature was the only sorceress,
And passion all the magic that we knew —
Siward and I, bewitching and bewitched.
I loved him ere I saw him, hearing told
The story of his prowess, while his name
On eager tongues o'er-ran the murmuring street.
Like one who sickens till the judge pronounce
Immediate life or death, pulseless I watched
His crowded passage : had he not looked up
I think I should have died; but our eyes met ;
Our souls saluted proudly, swift to guess
How great a thing had happened in the world —

   Ermengarde.   How great a thing!

   Godfrida.   Was it not great indeed
That we two for each other made and marked
Should thus encounter — he, out of the North,
A casual roving visitant ; and I
A southern home-bird?   Kneel with me — kneel down,

                               [Kneels.]

All gentle people, and implore her Grace
To thwart no love decreed by destiny
Like mine and Siward's — a surpassing love,
Most strangely sprung to perfect life, a thing

To tell of always, beautiful and great ! —
Will no one help ?

   Isembert.   Your witchcraft fails you here.
You are upon your knees ; confess your crime,
And beg her Grace's pardon.

                    [GODFRIDA *springs to her feet.*]
                        No ! — the law
Condemns the sorceress to die by fire.
Are you determined to be burned alive ?

   Godfrida.   No ! [*In a piercing voice.*] Siward !
      Siward !

      SIWARD *in* THANGBRAND'S *dress enters the gal-
      lery unseen by any one on the stage.* ANSELM
      re-enters by the door on the right.

   Isembert.   Till the spell be broken
You shall not see him. Would you, while you burn,
Behold him looking on, or would you live
A free maid once again ? Godfrida, choose.

   Godfrida. I have no choice. Siward and I are one.

   Isembert [*to* ERMENGARDE]. For your old friendship's
      sake, and since her soul
Seems powerless to repent, by gentle means
Let us deliver her if it may be.
Were she to wed some worthy man, I think
The sinful charm might end.

Ermengarde.   I think it might.

Isembert.   Not long ago she loved Sir Adomar;
And he returned her love.   Let them be —

  Godfrida.   Shame !

Adomar !   [*Looks about.*]   Adomar ! — I saw him here.

    [*She catches* ADOMAR'S *eye, and he comes for-
        ward reluctantly.*]

Answer me, sir, as if I were the judge
Of all things.   Did I ever make you think
By word or glance, by any faintest sign,
That you were more to me than one I knew?

  Adomar.   Never.   [*Turns back into the crowd.*

  Isembert.   He wore your ribbon.

  Godfrida.   Adomar !

My ribbon, sir, how came it to be yours?

                                [*He faces* GODFRIDA.

  Adomar.   By chance.

  Godfrida.   Say when.

  Adomar.   It was no fault of mine.

He had a ribbon too; and so had he —
And he — and he: I could not help myself.
Godfrida's ribbon fell to me by lot
Upon the morning of St. Valentine.

  Isembert.   But why are you the only pair whose names
Were coupled when the sport that joined them ceased?

Godfrida. Answer! [*Keeps her eyes fixed on* ADOMAR.

Adomar.   Because I wore her ribbon still;
And talked of marrying her; and bragged — and talked.

Isembert. On what pretence?

Adomar.   Because I thought . . . because
I am a fool, I fear.

Godfrida.   An honest one!

Isembert. Did you desire to marry her?

Adomar.   I did.

Isembert. And do you now?

Adomar.   No.

Isembert.   Why not, Adomar?

Adomar. Sometimes I thought she was too slight for
     me,
Because she seemed so simple and so sweet;
But knowing now how great her spirit is,
And since she seems — [*To* GODFRIDA] I pray you,
     pardon me —
A witch, I fear I am no mate for her.

                    [*Returns into the crowd.*

Isembert. Is not this witchcraft? Here is Adomar,
The very vainest man in all Provence,
Professing poverty of soul, because
Godfrida eyed him closely. It must end.
And as she will not marry Adomar,

And he refuses her, she shall be matched
Beneath her rank; for Siward must be loosed
From her malignant power immediately.

Ermengarde.   Marry her to a beggar from the streets.

Isembert.   It shall be done !   Godfrida, ere we send
To fetch your husband, will you break the spell,
Confess and be forgiven?

> [GODFRIDA *is stunned; the bystanders are much*
> *moved, and ominous glances are cast at* ISEM-
> BERT.]   Choose again.

The choice is threefold : freedom, death by fire,
Or marriage with a beggar.

Ermengarde.   What ? — She spoke ?

Isembert.   Her heart is vexed beyond the power of
words. —

Anselm, go quickly to the street; bring in
The first man you encounter; rich or poor,
Base-born or noble, she shall marry him,
If he be single and will have her.   Haste !

> [ANSELM *goes out by the door on the right and*
> SIWARD *leaves the gallery.*]

The sight of him whose hand can rescue her
From burning may decide her preference.

Godfrida.   Madam, you loved me once . . . What
can I say?

Is there no pity anywhere? No help?
Hush! That's not right! There was a word I had:
Sweetly and valiantly! Yes! I am his:
And you can never sever from my soul
The soul of Siward, mine in life, in death.

> [*Unsheathes a dagger which she wears in her belt.*
> ANSELM *ushers in* SIWARD *by the door on the*
> *right.* SIWARD'S *hat hides his face.* GOD-
> FRIDA *is the first to recognise him. Dropping*
> *her dagger she rushes silently into his arms.*
> *As she approaches him* SIWARD *throws off*
> *his hat.*

Voices. Siward! — Long life to Siward and Godfrida!

> [ISEMBERT, *quickly concealing his discomfiture,*
> *rises and faces* ERMENGARDE, *who has also*
> *risen in fear and anger.*

Isembert. I am guiltless here. Chance is too strong
for us.

Enter LUDOVIC *by the large door, accompanied by* Men-
at-arms. *They push their way through the crowd to*
the front.

Ludovic. Madam, a messenger, arrived but now
Declares Esplandian has crossed the Rhone,
And marches on St. Andiol.

Isembert.   I know.

You had my mandate to prepare for war?

Ludovic.   And I obeyed.

Isembert.   When can our troops set out?

Ludovic.   Now.

Isembert.   Admirable! You shall lead them. Go.

Captains and Men-at-arms.   No! Siward! Siward!

Ludovic.   Siward, I say too.

Isembert.   That cannot be.

Voices.   Siward! Siward must lead!

Ermengarde [*demoralised by the clamour*]. Let Siward
     lead.

Voices.   Give him his sword again!

Ermengarde [*to* GAUCELM].   Bring me his sword.

Isembert [*delaying* GAUCELM *with a gesture*].   But
     our revenge?

Ermengarde.   At once!

          [GAUCELM *goes out by the door on the left.*]

I cannot face an outraged people.   You —

Speak to them, reconcile them, Isembert.

Isembert [*reluctantly, to* SIWARD].   Her Grace re-
     stores your freedom and command.

Siward.   I thank her Grace; but neither will I
     have

Unless Godfrida be released.

Voices.   Right, sir!

Long live Godfrida! Set her free, your Grace!

Ermengarde [*in a choking voice*]. I set her free. —
　　Speak for me, Isembert!

[*Frantically.*] It was his doing: I am not to blame!

　　[*Sinks into her chair, wringing her hands in fear
　　and shame.*

Re-enter GAUCELM *with* SIWARD'S *sword. He offers it
　　to the Duchess, but* ISEMBERT *takes it.*

Voices. Down with him! Villain! Death to Isembert!

Isembert. Good friends, and noble foes — since both
　　are here —

Voices. All foes!

Isembert.   All foes, then! On myself I take
Whatever culpability may be
In these proceedings; but condemn me not
Unheard. My scrupulous, unselfish aim
Contemplated the service of Provence
In liberating Siward from a bond
Which I believed, and honestly believed,
A danger to the state, knowing that war
Knocked at our gates again.

Voices.   A lie! A lie!

Down with the upstart!. Death to Isembert!

[ISEMBERT *endeavours to secure silence by his lofty and patient bearing; but as the clamour continues, he at last throws his glove on the stage, and the shouting ceases.* SIWARD *lifts the glove.*

Isembert.   Take my defiance, then!

Siward.   Our private feuds
Must wait until we conquer outward peace.

Isembert.   Then — now — at any time I will maintain
Against the world that this malicious witch
Corrupted Siward and deserves to die!

Siward.   Unhallowed liar!

Isembert [*returning his sword to* SIWARD].   Your
sword, Sir Constable.

ACT-DROP *rapidly.*

7

ACT IV.

SCENE.— *Theodoric's Tower. The ruins of a Gothic castle situated on the crest of a low hill. A mouldering ivy-covered wall stretches obliquely from right to left. The wall decreases in height toward the left, and is finally broken away, showing the ridge crowned in the near distance by a tower. On the left down to the front are trees : on the right, a gateway and a few trees. In the middle of the wall is a large window about three feet from the ground; the ivy grows all round and outside the window. On the extreme right is a low doorway in the wall. Near the centre of the stage a fragment of masonry to serve as a seat. Behind and over the wall the sky alone is visible. There are five entrances : by the window in the centre; by the low doorway on the right; by the gateway; and an upper and lower left entrance.*

It is evening when the act opens, and the sun has sunk by the end of it.

On the rising of the act-drop INGLERAM *is standing at the window and* DAGOBERT *is looking out on the left.*

With the exception of ANSELM, *in this act all the men are armed according to their rank.*

Ingleram [turning to DAGOBERT]. Well, and I care not who knows it, I would sooner watch a battle from this window, than have the whole credit of gaining one.

Enter CYPRIAN, *lower left.*

Dagobert. Have you seen Berthold?

Cyprian. I passed him on my way hither. Adomar had him in his clutches.

Ingleram [who has crossed to the left]. Here comes Berthold — with Adomar. We shall never get rid of the fool. [*Comes down stage. They stand close together.*] Are we agreed? Is the signal understood?

Dagobert. Yes; when the battle is about to begin, Esplandian's trumpets shall sound retreat, and in the amazement and confusion of this we change sides.

Ingleram. And we four together charge Siward.

Cyprian. How many men have you?

Dagobert. Why, half the army is with us in spirit. The rank and file hate the Norseman and his tight rein.

Cyprian. But have you no list of names? I trust only acknowledged traitors.

Dagobert. Oh, yes! some hundreds.

Cyprian. And these will go over compactly in the sight of both armies?

Dagobert. Yes.

   Enter BERTHOLD *and* ADOMAR, *upper left.*

Adomar [*before and as he enters*]. Now, for my part, sorcery is one of those things that a man may very well consider twice or thrice before —

Ingleram. Berthold, we had some words yesterday — your hand.

Berthold. I have forgotten.

Ingleram. In the palace.

Berthold. No; my memory is like an empty sponge, and my head aches like a beaten anvil. Adomar, tell them the news.

Adomar. Why, gentlemen, the Duchess has come into the camp with a bevy of ladies. They have watched Siward carry all before him in the lists — including me. Now they wish to see him win a battle. And here they will take their stand.

Ingleram. Ay, ay, Adomar! Well, since the Duchess is the prize for which Esplandian fights, it is fitting she should be in evidence.

Adomar. Yes. But do you know what Isembert is saying?

Ingleram. No, Adomar.

Adomar. He says that I have developed a fine vein of irony — which was unsuspected in me.

Ingleram. Ah!

Adomar. But is your niece really a sorceress, Ingleram?

Ingleram. Oh yes! like all handsome ladies. The vein of irony, Adomar; show us the splinter that pleased Isembert.

Adomar. Why, it was thus. The Duchess asked me to marry Godfrida, but I said, "No; seeing she is so high-spirited, I perceive I am no mate for her." [*They stare at him blankly.*] Well, Isembert thinks it highly ironical. I didn't mean it, of course; but I said it: you see Godfrida looked at me so fixedly I spoke without thinking.

Cyprian. That is how the truth always leaks out.

Adomar. Is irony truth?

Dagobert [*pointing to the left*]. Look! Siward with Ludovic and those of his person.

> [GODFRIDA *enters on the right, and seeing her uncle goes out immediately.*]

Berthold. They are coming this way.

Ingleram. No; I think not. They can observe the enemy as well where they are.

Berthold. We have a better view here.

Ingleram.   Let us slip past them.   The trees will screen us.

Adomar.   Isembert said it was irony.   He said I must have meant it ironically, and I believe Isembert.

Cyprian.   Stick to that, Adomar.

　　　　　　　[*All except* ADOMAR *go out by lower left.*

Adomar.   Yes; but don't you also think it highly ironical?　　　　　　　　　　　[*About to go out.*

　　　Re-enter GODFRIDA *on the right.*

Godfrida.   Adomar!   Adomar!

Adomar.   Godfrida!

Godfrida.   Help me, Adomar.   Tell Siward I am here.

Adomar.   Tell Siward!—Yes; but why not go to him yourself?

Godfrida.   It must not be known that I have come, unless Siward sanctions my presence.   See that no one hears you but Siward.   Quickly, I beg you, Adomar.

　　　[ADOMAR *goes out upper left.*   GODFRIDA, *screen-*
　　　　　ing herself behind the trees, looks out left for
　　　　　several seconds; then with a gesture of de-
　　　　　light crosses to the window.

　　　　　Enter SIWARD, *upper left.*

Godfrida.   Siward!

Siward.　　　　　　Godfrida!

Godfrida.　　　　　　　　　　I have come to you!

Siward.   Alone ?

Godfrida.   Alone.

Siward.   · On foot?

Godfrida.   On Pericles,
My palfrey.   In a wood I tethered him
A mile away : if I had ridden here
I might have been discovered by my foe
Ere I had seen you.   Will she send me back?
Oh, may I stay?

Siward.   My word is here supreme !
And stay you shall, most gallant wanderer.

Godfrida.   Who, if not I, should see you in the field ?
Let me not hinder you.   Where shall I go?

Siward.   The battle is not yet.

Godfrida.   When will it be ?

Siward.   I cannot tell.   I wait to be attacked.

Godfrida.   But is it brave to wait ?

Siward.   Sometimes it is.
Courage endures vexation and delay,
Biding its time while frantic cowardice
Leaps to unlooked-for ruin.   Timid souls
Are always in a hurry.

Godfrida.   Am I then
A timid soul?   I hurried; I was vexed.
I thought how other ladies watching you

Would quail and flush again with fear and joy,
And jealous of them all I took the road.

Siward. Out of your shining eyes your brave soul leans
As from your lattice once your body bent;
You are all light and fragrance, fire and dew.

Godfrida. Oh, as I galloped hither, in my ears
The rushing wind like war-trumps sang! I heard
The snap of riven lances, and the clash
Of blades, the thudding mace, extorted cries,
Deep groans and stifled breath!—drums, cymbals, bells;
And in a flashing vision you I saw
Order the battle horsed on victory.

Siward [*pre-occupied. Pointing through the window*].

The victory will be thrust upon our hands:
Esplandian cannot wait. He shifts his front;
Moves here and there, extends this wing or that,
Until his army like a restive horse
Unaptly managed, plunges desperately.
Here you can watch the fight. Now I must go.

Godfrida. Let me go with you. Just a little way.

[*They go out upper left.*

Enter ERMENGARDE, ISEMBERT, LUDOVIC, ANSELM, *and*
Lieutenant, *with* Ladies, Maids-of-Honour *and* Halberdiers.

Ermengarde. He is not here.

Ludovic.   Madam, he went this way.

Adomar came for him.

> [ISEMBERT, *looking out upper left, points out* SI-
> WARD *and* GODFRIDA *to* ERMENGARDE, *who
> then comes down to the centre of the stage and
> sits, holding her hand to her heart. Her
> maids come about her with assistance, but she
> motions them away.*

Ermengarde.   Leave me awhile.

[*All go out except* ISEMBERT, *and he is about to follow.*

Not all alone. [ISEMBERT *stands beside her.*] — I should

    have burned the witch !

The brilliant day a smoky hovel seems

While she free-hearted breathes. Oh, Isembert,

Can nothing help me now ?

Isembert [*with disdain*].   A steadfast will ;

That always can avail. Clasp to your mind

The reason why you set Godfrida free :

Your Duchy was at stake, and Siward's sword

Your only hope : you dared not thwart his love.

Ermengarde.   I care not for my Duchy ! I was faint

With rending passions, and my memory

Oblivious of the true alternative —

Her life or mine. Counsel me now again.

Isembert. They are not married yet.

Ermengarde [*rises eagerly*].   True, Isembert!
What then, my friend?

Isembert.   Nothing, except that chance
Is active in the world.

Ermengarde.   The chance of war?

Isembert.   A thousand things may happen.

Ermengarde.   Certainly!
Siward may fall.   That would not be amiss.
I hate him while I love him.

Isembert.   Love is blind
Until it learns to hate the thing it loves.

Ermengarde.   Godfrida . . . Isembert!   The chance
of war!
Godfrida — she might fall!

Isembert.   Hardly by chance.

Ermengarde.   But it might seem to be!   If she were
dead,
Out of her grave my life would grow again!
Her life or mine!   Oh, you can help me now!

Isembert.   The chance of war?   The license of the
camp:
The sutler's men; the rabble — murderers
Among them; robbers, bravos.   Killed? — and robbed? —
But Siward would not love you.

Ermengarde.   What of that!

It matters little now who has his love,

If this one hated creature be not she.

Oh, will you understand a woman's heart!

She was my rival, and she baffled me.

    Isembert.   If I devise Godfrida's murder, think

Whose death would follow quickly.

    Ermengarde.   Whose, then?

    Isembert.   Mine.

You see, I understand one woman's heart.

    Ermengarde.   What! I would have you killed?

    Isembert.   Infallibly.

    Ermengarde.   Because I would be in your power?

    Isembert.   Even so.

    Ermengarde.   You understand me not at all, my
        friend. —

Who knows my subtle brain, my fiery soul?

Nay, I remember all your adoration!

Oh, if you love me let Godfrida die!

    Isembert.   And afterwards? How soon should my
        time come?

    Ermengarde.   When it should please you.

    Isembert.   Please me?

    Ermengarde.   If my life

Be by her death preserved — and in her death

Alone lies hope for me! — I owe my life.

Isembert.   Your life?

Ermengarde.   Myself.

Isembert.   You owe yourself to me?

Ermengarde.   It would amaze the world! But we
should stir

Amazement more profound; for we have brains.

What could we not accomplish, Isembert?

We 'd make Provence a kingdom once again!

Isembert.   You mean to marry me — to be my wife?

Ermengarde.   If you will have so deeply scorned a gift
As my poor broken heart.

> [*Watching* ERMENGARDE *closely,* ISEMBERT *kisses
> her hand, and then her cheek.*

Isembert.   By chance of war.

Ermengarde.   My wounds begin to heal.

> [*A confused noise of voices is heard from the left.*

Isembert.   What is it now?

[*Re-enter by the lower left* LUDOVIC, Lieutenant *and* Hal-
berdiers *with* MARCABRUN *and* MELCHIOR. *The*
Ladies *crowd in the entrance.* MARCABRUN *and*
MELCHIOR *are dressed in rags and rusty armour.
They carry long-swords; and have the appearance of
thorough scoundrels.*]

Who are these, Ludovic?

Ludovic.   They look like spies.

We found them lurking in a thicket near.

Isembert. Most problematic rogues! Leave them to me.

Ermengarde [*affecting gaiety*].   Come, let us find our
amorous general.

> [ERMENGARDE, LUDOVIC, ANSELM, *and the* Ladies
> *go out by the upper left.*

Isembert [*to* MARCABRUN *and* MELCHIOR].   Come
here. [*To* Lieutenant.]   Stand aside.   [Lieutenant *and*
Halberdiers *draw off, and the* Spadassins *approach* ISEM-
BERT, *who is seated.*]   What are you?

Melchior.   We are poor fellows, sir.

Isembert.   You look like crafty rascals.   Are you spies?

Marcabrun.   Oh, no, sir!   Crafty rascals, but not spies.

Melchior.   There's no deceiving you, sir.   We are
Provençals.

Isembert.   Of what town?

Melchior.   Saddlers of Aix, sir.

Isembert.   And why have you left your work?

Marcabrun.   It left us, sir.

Isembert.   You must not lie to me.   You robbed your
masters and decamped.   You are thieves, human vul-
tures, come hither to strip the dead.   And I suspect you
of another trade.   These long-swords.   If a man had an
enemy, now?

Melchior. What do you take us for?

Marcabrun. For cut-throats, to be sure! He has an enemy.

Isembert. What if I had an enemy?

[*He rises, and the three draw close together.*

Marcabrun. For ten broad pieces you could say indeed, "I had an enemy."

Isembert. Both of you shall have a score of broad pieces.

Melchior. In hand?

Isembert. Five in hand. The rest when the deed is done.

Melchior. Ten in hand.

Isembert. Five in hand; or you shall hang off-hand.

Marcabrun. Let it be. — When and where shall we receive the balance?

Isembert. Be at the gate of the Cathedral of Arles to-morrow by sunset.

Marcabrun. Who shall bring it?

Isembert. I, or another.

Marcabrun. Who are you, sir?

Isembert. That is not in the bargain. — I shall keep you under arrest in the meantime. When I set you free, you must hide in my neighbourhood. After the battle joins, seeming to fly in terror, you shall observe a lady standing beside me on my left.

Marcabrun. Observe a lady standing on your left.

Isembert. Your swords are in your hands as you rush past.

Marcabrun. And being beside ourselves with fear we might in our panic wound the lady.

Isembert. Death.

Marcabrun. Kill her outright by one of those untoward accidents. — And afterwards?

Isembert. Continue your flight. Save yourselves.

[*The pair move a little aside and consult in whispers.*

Marcabrun. On your left, sir?

Isembert. On my left.

    [*The pair agree together, and hold out their hands
      to* ISEMBERT.

[*Giving money.*] I shall seem to repel your attack; but heed nothing I may do or say.

Marcabrun. It is understood, sir.

Melchior. Unless we see a clear way of escape we harm no one, remember.

Isembert. That also is understood. [*Recalls* Lieutenant.] Resume your charge. These are not spies. Proceed.

    [Lieutenant *and* Halberdiers *march* MARCABRUN
      and MELCHIOR *out lower left.*

Isembert.   She means my death: she could not marry
   me!
Yet stranger things have been . . . I kissed her cheek.
Would mere dissimulation suffer that? . . .
I'll play the great game as it should be played:
There is one way alone — the way to win.

> [*Kettle-drums are heard from the valley. Re-
> enter* Lieutenant *with* MARCABRUN, MEL-
> CHIOR, *and* Halberdiers.

Well?
   Lieutenant.   The Duchess is returning, sir.
   Isembert [*takes* MARCABRUN *and* MELCHIOR *to the low
doorway at the back*].   Down there; and see you do your
duty.   [MARCABRUN *and* MELCHIOR *go out.*

> *Re-enter* ERMENGARDE *lower left.*

   Isembert.   Esplandian descends into the plain.
   Ermengarde.   As Siward said he would. — Is it
prepared?
   Isembert.   Yes.
   Ermengarde.   Shall I see it?
   Isembert.   Yes, if you look on.
   Ermengarde.   I spoke to her — Oh! civilly enough! —
Her senses reel with love and pride.   She comes
To watch the battle here.

Isembert. And that is well,

For she must stand by me.

Ermengarde. I shall take care.

Isembert [*indicating* Halberdiers]. These must be
further off.

Ermengarde. Appoint their place.

Isembert. Station yourselves among the cypresses.

[Lieutenant *and* Halberdiers *are about to file out,
upper left, when* GODFRIDA *and* ANSELM
enter quickly, and cross to the window.
Maids-of-Honour *and* Ladies *enter, some
upper and some lower left, and look over
the wall where it is lowest. The* Halberdiers
*go out, but re-enter when the trumpet sounds
and look over the wall among the ladies.*
ERMENGARDE, *standing near the centre of the
stage, watches* GODFRIDA. ISEMBERT, *near
the front, on the left, watches the whole scene.*

Anselm [*seated in the window*]. I cannot see him yet.

Godfrida. There, Anslem! Look!

He rides to battle!

Anselm. And I am dangling here

Among the women on a ruined wall!

I have no chance, Godfrida!

Godfrida. You shall see

8

Your hero triumph.   Is not that enough?
The sky broods over him; the breathless winds
Are listening: when the silver clarions sound
Siward shall gather victory like a rose.

> [*A trumpet sounds from the valley.*

Ermengarde [*rushes to the window*].   What's that?

Isembert [*goes to the window*].   A note of truce or of
    retreat!
Our troops go over to the enemy!

Ermengarde.   What! my Provençals! God, I cannot
    look!

> [*Comes down stage and sinks on the seat.*

Godfrida.   They strike at Siward!

Anselm.   Ah! he is betrayed!
They hem him round!   His own men turn against him!

Ermengarde.   Who leads the rebels?

Isembert.   Dagobert, I think.
They swarm and shift.   What! — No; I cannot tell.

> [*Comes down quickly to the front.*

[*To himself.*]   This was their plot then!   And my
    Cyprian
The foremost in it — sombre, subtle knave!

Godfrida.   But look at Siward, fighting!   See him
    there!
He makes a space about him!

Anselm.   Back to back,
Some one supports him! Thangbrand it must be.
I too shall help him!

                        [*Goes out by the window.*

Godfrida.   Go, my brave one ; go !
Tell Siward I am waiting for him here.

    Isembert [*at the front. To himself*]. On whose left
        shall I stand?

              If Siward falls
Godfrida might be mine. That I must watch.

              [*Goes quickly to the window.*

Is Siward down? I cannot see him now.

    Godfrida. I think he cut his way out of the
        throng.

    Isembert [*comes down to* ERMENGARDE]. Madam,
        you must determine —

    Ermengarde [*weakly*]. Let me be !

    Isembert [*comes down to the front. To himself*]. Prov-
        ence is doomed ! This feeble halting soul,
Aghast in her despair, would cling to me
With poverty and ruin for her dower.
The other woman, like a fount of hope,
Could help a beaten man to win the world.
On whose left shall I stand? The temptress there,
The woman who desires the other's death,

Deserves herself to die.   [ERMENGARDE *sobs.*]   Madam,
  I think
I 'd better put an end to your distress.

> [*A restless movement has been in progress among
> the* Halberdiers. *One or two have already
> stolen stealthily out.*

Lieutenant [*panic-stricken*].   Esplandian charges
  home; the game is up;
Our men on all sides fly!   Each for himself!

> [*Comes down to* ERMENGARDE.

Madam, you must with us.   Come!
Halberdiers.   Save yourselves!

> [*The panic becomes general.* Halberdiers *and*
> Ladies *rush out upper left.* One of the Hal-
> berdiers *drops his halbert.* ERMENGARDE
> *staggering to her feet picks it up.*

Ermengarde [*leaning on the halbert*].   Here shall I
  stay, and this shall guard me now!

> [Lieutenant *goes out upper left.*

You paltry coward!
Isembert [*to himself*].   So! some courage yet! . . .
The quaking murderers must now be near. . . .
Why should they kill at all?   I see no cause;
No end to serve, since Siward's overthrow
Destroys the world I make.   Or does some power

Abash my spirit? — I am purged of self!
Before the hurrying issue, life or death,
I have become impartial destiny:
I hold the balances; I must be just!
Neither shall die!

Re-enter MARCABRUN *and* MELCHIOR *by the low doorway
at the back, running with drawn swords. Seeing
ISEMBERT standing alone, they halt. ISEMBERT signs
to them to withdraw; but ERMENGARDE attacks them
frantically with the halbert.*

Ermengarde.   More cowards still! Go back!
Back! Would you live for ever? Back and fight!

[*The Spadassins defend themselves.* ISEMBERT
    running to ERMENGARDE'S *assistance gets
    upon her right.*

Isembert.   Hold, villains! Hold your hands!
Marcabrun and *Melchior.*   Upon your left!

[*They wound* ERMENGARDE *and run out on the
    right. The halbert falls from* ERMEN-
    GARDE'S *hands.* ISEMBERT *supports her, and*
    GODFRIDA *runs to her assistance.*

Ermengarde. Godfrida. [*Tries to push her away.*
    GODFRIDA *moves from her.*] Isembert, did they
    mistake?

My heart . . . Oh! Oh! . . . I should have burned
the witch.

Isembert.   Help her, Godfrida.

Godfrida.   No; my post is here.

Ermengarde.   The tournament is over. . . . Home, my
lords !

Godfrida.   Poor lady ! I will go a little way.

> [ISEMBERT *and* GODFRIDA *help* ERMENGARDE *out,*
> *lower left.*

Enter DAGOBERT, *upper left, meeting* INGLERAM *who*
enters, wounded, on the right.

Dagobert.   I cannot find him anywhere.

Ingleram.   Nor I.
Is that Godfrida ?

Dagobert.   Yes, with Isembert.
They help the Duchess hence.   Her reign is done.
Where are the others ?

Ingleram.   Berthold fell; I saw
The thirsty earth lap up the drunkard's life.

Dagobert.   But Cyprian?

Ingleram.   Wounded to death, he says.

Dagobert.   If Siward has escaped I'll find him yet.

> [*Goes out by the right.*

Ingleram.   And I'll find out a surgeon.   If this fop
Encounters Siward single-handed, why

Siward will slice him as I would a joint.

Berthold and Dagobert and Cyprian dead,

Old Ingleram 's the only gleaner left

After Esplandian's harvest in Provence !

I'll find a surgeon for old Ingleram —

A gentle surgeon for old Ingleram.

And for this damsel-errant niece of mine,

I'll yoke her with a husband speedily.

> [*Goes out upper left.*

Re-enter GODFRIDA *lower left. She crosses to the window and looks out. Then re-enter* ISEMBERT. *He stands for a moment, then goes to* GODFRIDA *and lays his hand on her shoulder.*

Isembert.   Godfrida.

Godfrida.   Leave me, sir.

Isembert.   The Duchess paid

Her life for yours.   I would have saved you both :

But malice, in the saddle, spurs a course

Uncurbed, although repentance leap behind. —

The past is done with ; here for us begins

Another age, another world.   Defeat,

Like death, opens the gate of life : my soul

Arises from the mouldering sepulchre

Of mean ambition, spotless to achieve

A new device, a cognizance divine.

I dedicate my life to you : no word
Of love, no hint, no glance shall trouble you :
You shall be high and sacred.   Come !

Godfrida.   I wait
On Siward.   I am his.

Isembert.   Siward is dead.

Godfrida.   He is not dead !   I saw death at his side
In ghostly armour like an angel fight
Against his foes.

[*Re-enter* SIWARD *by the window.   He has lost his helmet, but is unwounded.*]

                              If he be dead
Behold his radiant spirit !

Siward.   Isembert,
I underlie your challenge, and shall rob
The gallows of a villain. —   Quickly, sir.

Isembert [*choking*].   Devil !   who sends you here to
        damn my soul ?
Out of the earth an elemental hate
Invades my spirit at the sight of you,
Dethrones my newly crowned benevolence,
And hurls me at your throat, stark ruffian !
Now, for Godfrida !

Siward.   For Godfrida, sir !

                              [*They fight.*

Isembert.   Now ! now !

> [*He stumbles.*

Siward.   You 'll spit yourself upon my sword.
Take time ; take breath.

Isembert.   Your breath I mean to take !
He who in single combat conquers you,
The undefeated warrior, reaps your fame,
And on my brow I swear to set that wreath.

> [*Attacks* SIWARD.

Siward.   Not in this region was my conqueror born.

> [*He drives* ISEMBERT *towards the window.*

Isembert.   Now !   For Godfrida !   Now !   Help me,
   my heart !

> [*He is driven over the window mortally wounded,
> the word "* heart *" being prolonged into a des-
> pairing shriek.* SIWARD *crosses quickly to
> the right and listens intently.* GODFRIDA
> *looks fearfully over the window, and then
> runs to* SIWARD.

Godfrida.   Unsparing death ! most terrible it seems !
Must we die too ?

Siward.   Yes ; when our time shall come ;
Not now.

Godfrida.   But, Siward, Ermengarde is dead.

Siward.   How did she die ?

Godfrida.   By treachery.   I fear
She fell upon the swords she aimed at me.

Siward.   Treason on every hand — a pestilence
Inherent in the air! — They come? — Not yet!

Godfrida.   Who come?

Siward.   My horses.   Thangbrand
      brings them up,
And Anselm.   Hearts of gold!   They will not fail:
When Thangbrand sounds his horn the way is clear.

Godfrida.   Betrayed and hunted, why are you so glad,
So like a conqueror?

Siward.   And so I am!
I cleft a passage through a hundred foes!
Each nerve and sinew, every sounding pulse
That marks the tramp of life along my veins
Is charged to do my will triumphantly.
Anselm shall guide us safe to Avignon,
And there we shall be married.

Godfrida.   When?

Siward.   To-morrow.
Knight-errant and his lady, we shall ride
Across the plains of France, home to the north
Where kindly cold can temper human hearts,
And faith unflinching welds the souls of men.

Godfrida.   Our souls are welded.

Siward [*taking both her hands*].   Will you come
   with me?

Godfrida.   Now, as I am.   Take me to life or death.

Siward.   The way is long.

Godfrida.   My love will never end.

Siward.   I have no friend, no fortune but my sword.

Godfrida.   I bring you nothing — nothing but my love.

Siward.   Peril shall haunt our steps.

Godfrida.   Peril is wine :
I know its exaltation!

Siward.   Calumny
May overcast your fame.

Godfrida.   Not in your thought !
You cannot frighten me.   I am your mate !

Siward.   My mate? my queen !
   [*The low note of a bugle is heard on the right.*]
   The signal ! — Think again.
Godfrida, will you, dare you follow me?

Godfrida.   Sweetly and valiantly through all the
   world.

CURTAIN.